The Marquis of Stowe meets the beautiful Lady Burnham secretly in Grosvenor Chapel to learn that her husband is threatening divorce proceedings.

In a wild effort to prevent the scandal this will evoke he decides to offer marriage to the Duke of Dawlish's daughter, and leaves for the country.

On his way he encounters an accident and makes the acquaintance of Ajanta Tiverton, the beautiful daughter of a local Vicar. The Duke's daughter is so plain and dull that the Marquis, fighting to preserve his freedom, asks Ajanta to have a 'pretend' engagement with him until Lord Burnham is no longer suspicious.

How Ajanta and her family are swept into a rich, luxurious world they have never known before, how Lord Burnham faces them with an unexpected and frightening ultimatum, is told in this 302nd book by Barbara Cartland.

For All Eternity
Barbara Cartland

CORGI BOOKS
A DIVISION OF TRANSWORLD PUBLISHERS LTD

FOR ALL ETERNITY

A CORGI BOOK 0 552 12009 X

First publication in Great Britain

PRINTING HISTORY
Corgi edition published 1982

This book is set in 10/11 English Times

Corgi Books are published by
Transworld Publishers Ltd.,
Century House, 61–63 Uxbridge Road,
Ealing, London, W5 5SA

Made and printed in Great Britain by
Cox & Wyman Ltd., Reading.

Made and printed in United States of America by
Offset Paperbacks, Dallas, Pennsylvania.

ABOUT THE AUTHOR

Barbara Cartland, the world's most famous romantic novelist, who is also an historian, playwright, lecturer, political speaker and television personality, has now written over 300 books and sold over 300 million over the world.

She has also had many historical works published and has written four autobiographies as well as the biographies of her mother and that of her brother, Ronald Cartland, who was the first Member of Parliament to be killed in the last war. This book has a preface by Sir Winston Churchill and has just been republished with an introduction by Sir Arthur Bryant.

She has recently completed a novel, 'Love at the Helm' with the help and inspiration of the late Admiral of the Fleet, the Earl Mountbatten of Burma. This is being sold for the Mountbatten Memorial Trust.

Miss Cartland in 1978 sang an Album of Love Songs with the Royal Philharmonic Orchestra.

In 1976 by writing twenty-one books, she broke the world record and has continued for the following five years with 24, 20, 23, 24 and 24. In the Guinness Book of Records she is listed as the world's top-selling authoress.

In private life Barbara Cartland, who is a Dame of the Order of St. John of Jerusalem, Chairman of the St. John Council in Hertfordshire and Deputy President of the St. John Ambulance Brigade, has fought for better conditions and salaries for Midwives and Nurses.

She has championed the cause for old people, had the law altered regarding gypsies and founded the first

Romany Gypsy camp in the world.

Barbara Cartland is deeply interested in Vitamin Therapy and is President of the National Association for Health.

She has a magazine: 'Barbara Cartland's World of Romance' now being published in the U.S.A. and 'Barbara Cartland's Romantic World Tours operate from America in conjunction with BRITISH AIRWAYS.

AUTHOR'S NOTE

Divorce in England at the time of this story had to go through Parliament, who like other Protestant countries, alone had the power to dissolve marriages.

Such private acts were however difficult to obtain and so extremely expensive that only the wealthiest could contemplate them.

The total number of Parliamentary divorces for over 350 years between 1602 and 1859 were 317.

For a lady to be divorced was to incur complete ostracism. Those who were, immediately fled abroad and never returned. A gentleman however was soon forgiven although he was not always reinstated in Court circles.

The appellation *'a blue stocking'* derives from the blue worsted stockings worn by Edward Stilling Fleet, grandson of the famous Bishop of Worcester. He was so poor that when he attended the literary salons of Mrs. Edward Montague, 1720–1800, in Portman Square, he could not afford the correct black silk stockings which should have been worn with his knee breeches.

CHAPTER ONE

1818

"I am – sorry," Lady Burnham said.

The Marquis of Stowe did not reply. He only stared ahead, not seeing the high stained-glass window over the altar, or the finely painted reredos.

Instead he was seeing the scandal and the humiliation which made him shrink in horror from the contemplation of what it would mean.

How, he asked himself, could he have been so foolish or so blind as not to realise that Lord Burnham, who had always disliked him, would if he got the opportunity, take his revenge.

They had, as two members of the same Club, insulted each other subtly and wittily on every possible occasion.

They had challenged each other with their race-horses on every race-course, and while it had amused him to have a secret *affaire de coeur* with Lord Burnham's wife, His Lordship had now a weapon in his hand which he would not hesitate to use.

"I do not – know how it – could have – happened – how we can have been – watched without our being – aware of – it," Leone Burnham said with tears in her voice.

She was very lovely, and at any other time and place her distress and her broken little sobs would have made any man she was with want to comfort her.

But the Marquis's lips were set in a tight line and his chin was square as he went on staring blindly ahead of him and made no reply.

"I have lain awake all night – wondering who George's informant could be," Lady Burnham went on. "I always – believed the servants were – loyal to me rather than to him as he is very sharp with them."

Still the Marquis did not speak and she continued as if speaking to herself:

"I suppose he must have employed somebody to – follow us, but surely we should have – noticed him, or perhaps it was – somebody in your employment."

The Marquis thought this might be the explanation. After all, however much he trusted his servants there were always those who could be bribed if the money offered was large enough.

"What did your husband say he was going to do?" he asked, feeling as if the words were forced from between his lips.

They were both talking in lowered voices because of the place in which they had met.

The Marquis had hardly been able to believe it when he received a note early this morning saying:

"Something terrible has happened. I must see you immediately! Meet me in the Grosvenor Chapel in one hour's time."

At first he thought it must be a joke, then he not only recognised Leone's handwriting, but was told by his valet it had been brought to his house by a middle-aged woman who had been there before.

The Marquis knew this was Lady Burnham's maid whom she trusted implicitly with the notes that passed between them, and who was the only person who was aware of the assignations they made and how often they saw each other.

Knowing that going to the Grosvenor Chapel meant he would have to forgo his usual ride in the Park, the Marquis however had obeyed Lady Burnham's command and entered the Chapel somewhat apprehensively.

Situated in South Audley Street he was aware that it was almost directly behind the elegant house which the Burnhams occupied in Park Street. It would therefore be possible for Lady Burnham to tell her household she was going to Church and she would be able to walk there without being escorted by a footman.

He glanced around thinking that perhaps the whole thing was a hoax, then saw her sitting in a dark corner wearing for her, very unobtrusive clothes which made her seem shadowy and insubstantial.

He walked towards her and knew by the expression in her eyes before she spoke that something terrible, as she said, had happened.

He had anticipated what this might be before she actually put it into words, and now almost as if he must cling to every straw of hope which might save them from destruction he waited to hear exactly what had occurred.

"I knew as – soon as I saw George that he was in a bad – temper," Lady Burnham was saying, "but that is – nothing new – and as he did not kiss me, I was sure by the – expression in his eyes that – something was – very wrong."

She gave a little sob and wiped away a tear before she went on:

"He stood with his back to the fireplace and said:

" 'Well, I have caught you out and you can tell that stuck-up swine that I am taking my case to Parliament!' "

There was a moment's pause before she added a little incoherently:

"I think I – screamed. I only know I – asked him what he was – talking about.

" 'You know damned well what I was saying,' George replied, 'and if you think I am going to be cuckolded by a man I have always hated, you are very much mistaken! I am divorcing you, Leone, and citing him as co-respondent.' "

The Marquis did not speak. In fact he sat completely

immobile, almost as if he was turned to stone.

Only as Lady Burnham sobbed into her handkerchief and appeared to have nothing else to say did he ask:

"I presume you denied such charges?"

"Of course I did," she replied, "I told George he was – mad to believe such – things against me – but he would – not listen.

" 'I have irrefutable evidence,' he said, 'and there is nothing you or Stowe can say to deny it.' "

There was silence. Then she said again:

"I am sorry – Quintus, so very – very sorry!"

The Marquis was sorry too, for himself and for Leone Burnham.

He was well aware that if she was divorced she would be ostracised by every Lady of Quality in the land.

If he married her, and there was no doubt he would have to behave honourably as a Gentleman should, while he would be accepted in sporting and some social circles, she would be completely and irrevocably barred.

It was unfair, but the social code was very unbending where a woman was concerned, while it was generally accepted that a man might be promiscuous and get away with it.

"What evidence has your husband got?" he asked after a long silence and the only sound in the Chapel was Leone's sobs.

"It can only be the – times we have – met and – where," Lady Burnham replied in a broken voice. "You have never written me any – love-letters, and your notes, which I always – complained were very – impersonal, I burned – immediately I had – read them."

"You are sure of that?"

"Absolutely – sure!"

The Marquis thought there was one thing in his favour, that he had not been such a fool as to put his feelings down on paper.

At the same time, he was well aware that when the Earl

had been away he had, on several occasions, taken Leone through the garden-door into Stowe House late at night.

He had been quite sure at the time that nobody had seen them, but he had obviously been mistaken.

Because he had a rooted objection to making love in another man's bed he had never been so indiscreet as to go back to Burnham House.

But they had been fellow guests at house-parties where it had been accepted that their bedrooms should be near to each other, and on quite a number of occasions they had dined in a private room in places which offered accommodation for those who had no wish to be seen.

Leone had always worn a veil and they had slipped in surreptitiously through a conveniently placed side-entrance. It was an unwritten rule that clients who patronised the Restaurants in question never had their identities revealed.

But on the other hand, who could be sure that a waiter was not prepared to take a number of golden guineas to describe a Lady and a Gentleman he had served?

Or that a door-keeper had not gossiped with an ingratiating stranger who plied him with drink when he was off duty?

It would have been all too easy, the Marquis decided, if he had been doing the investigating rather than Lord Burnham, and he cursed himself for not being more astute and on his guard, especially when he was dealing with an avowed enemy.

"What can we – do?" Lady Burnham asked. "Is there – anything we can – do?"

"I am trying to think," the Marquis replied.

"Save me – please – save me, Quintus!" she begged. "You know I love you deeply – and you are the most attractive man I have ever met in the whole of my life. At the – same time how can I be – branded as – a 'Scarlet Woman'?"

She choked over the word, then went on pathetically:

15

"It means I shall never be asked to Balls and parties again, and shall never be able to go to – Court – or be allowed in the – Royal Enclosure at Ascot."

Her voice dropped to a whisper as she added:

"And you will soon grow bored with me as you have always with the others. Then I will want to – die! There would be – no point in going on – living!"

She was so distressed that at last the Marquis turned his head to look at her.

Despite her tear-stained face she was still lovely and he understood her misery.

"Stop crying – Leone," he said, "and let us think what we can do."

"You mean we will be able to – save ourselves?"

"I hope I can find a way of escaping from this morass into which we have fallen so foolishly."

"Oh, Quintus! If you can only do that – I will thank you from the – bottom of my heart."

"What did you finally say to your husband after he had told you he would divorce you?" the Marquis enquired.

"I went on protesting my – innocence, and said you were a – friend, and that we had done – nothing wrong."

"He obviously did not believe you."

"He is so – obsessed with the idea of revenge that he is determined to bring you down from your high perch, as he put it.

" 'I will teach Stowe, who with his airs and graces, thinks he is better than anybody else,' he said, 'a lesson he will not forget!' "

"And what did you reply?" the Marquis asked.

"I said: 'Even if you wish to hurt the Marquis, George, why should you wish to hurt me? I have done nothing – wrong?' "

"What did he reply to that?"

"He merely laughed a horrible vindictive laugh and went from the room."

"Did you see him again last night?"

16

Leone Burnham shook her head.

"He left the house, so I went to bed and cried."

There was a long silence. Then the Marquis said:

"I have an idea which might work."

"What is – it?"

She raised her face to his, but there was not much hope in her eyes which were wet with tears.

She was one of the beauties of London who had swept triumphantly aside all other aspirants for the title of 'Queen of Beauty'. But Lady Burnham at the moment looked crushed, miserable and insignificant.

The Marquis was still stiff as a ram-rod, his head held high, his chin square, as if he defied his foe and was prepared to fight to the death.

"I think," he said slowly as if he was thinking aloud before he spoke, "the only chance we have of convincing your husband that he was mistaken is if I immediately announce I am to be married."

Lady Burnham stared at him open-mouthed. Then she said:

"But, Quintus – I did not know you – intended to be – married. In fact, you have – always said . . ."

"Do not be stupid, Leone," the Marquis interrupted. "I am only telling you that if I announce my engagement before your husband has time to file his petition for a divorce, it would be more difficult for him to prove that I was at the same time pursuing you."

It took a second or two for Lady Burnham, who was not overintelligent, to understand what the Marquis was saying.

Then as she grasped it she replied:

"Of course! I see – what you mean. I could say that while we have been – together you were asking my – advice and I was – helping you to choose the girl who would make you a – suitable wife."

"Exactly!" the Marquis said dryly.

17

"But do you know of one? And even if you do, there will be no time to woo her."

The Marquis was well aware of that.

He had known Lord Burnham ever since they were at Eton together, and knew him to be a fiery, impetuous, uncontrolled character who would he was sure, if he had evidence that he considered conclusive, immediately rush ahead to bring his case before Parliament.

The only hope, since Parliament was never impulsive or in a hurry, was that all the preliminaries which involved Solicitors and clerks at the House would take days if not weeks to complete. With any luck the Marquis thought he might be able in that time to extricate himself from the mess he and Leone were in.

The Marquis had an extremely able and sharp brain when he wished to use it.

At this moment he knew he was fighting for the survival of everything that he valued in life.

He was very proud of his antecedents and very conscious that as head of the family he was looked up to and perhaps even revered by the other members of it.

He could imagine nothing more degrading than being involved in a divorce, the details of which would be broadcast to the public by being reported in the newspapers.

It was the kind of thing that the Marquis not only deplored when it happened to his contemporaries, but also he thought so vulgar and beneath him that he had never for one moment contemplated that it could become a personal problem.

It made him squirm even to think what the case would entail and the pity of his friends would be almost as hard to bear as the sneers and sniggers of his enemies.

Like a man in a trap he felt his brain was exploring every possible way of escape, but his instinct which had never before failed him in an emergency told him that this was the only possible way of avoiding catastrophe.

He was aware that Lady Burnham was looking at him with a flicker of hope in her eyes and the expression of a child who has been told at the last moment that she would not be punished as she had expected to be.

"Who is there who would – accept a proposal from you without – expecting a great deal of – preliminary attention?" she asked.

The Marquis knew she had grasped what he had been trying to say and was now asking the same questions as he was asking himself.

"I thought," he replied, "that young girls had their husbands chosen for them by their fathers."

"In noble families that is true," Lady Burnham agreed. "Papa was delighted when George asked if he could pay his addresses to me. But we had met at least half-a-dozen times before he did so, and he had made it very clear what his feelings were towards me."

"That was different because you are so beautiful," the Marquis said.

He made it sound not a compliment but the bare statement of a fact.

"Of course you are very important, Quintus," Lady Burnham said reflectively, "and I am sure the father of any débutante would be thrilled to have you as a son-in-law."

The Marquis knew this was true.

He had been angled after, cajolled, chased and pursued by every ambitious parent in the *Beau Monde* ever since leaving School.

Not only was his family one of the most distinguished in the country, but besides being an extremely wealthy man he was also handsome, talented and an acknowledged sportsman.

His detractors, and there were quite a number of them, however thought he was so puffed up with pride that it was impossible for him to look down at the toes of his Hessian boots.

They also called him autocratic, and when it suited them a tyrant. They even resented the fact that he was fully justified in being proud.

As if she was suddenly aware that the Marquis had so much to offer that, however swift and unexpected his courtship, nobody would be prepared to question it, Lady Burnham said quickly:

"Of course any girl would be lucky to have you as a husband. The only question is, who will it be?"

"I have decided that," the Marquis said.

"Who? Who is she?" Lady Burnham enquired.

She thought as she asked the question that she should be jealous, but somehow at the moment even the love which she had felt in the last months to be overwhelming seemed subordinate to the need for survival.

"I think that is something I should keep to myself," the Marquis answered.

He put out his hand as he spoke and took Lady Burnham's in his.

"Now listen, Leone," he said, "if I am to save you, and of course myself, we have to be very intelligent about it."

"Yes. .of – course."

Her fingers tightened on his and she clung to him as if he was a lifeline which would save her from drowning.

"I want you to go back to the house and insist upon seeing your husband," the Marquis went on. "Tell him you passed a sleepless night, unhappy and disturbed by his accusations."

"I understand – and I only – hope he will – listen to – me."

"You must make him listen!" the Marquis said firmly. "Tell him the reason why we have been seeing each other is that, since I thought it was time to settle down, I have been asking your advice as to who I should marry."

"I am – sure George will – never believe – me."

"Never mind. If he does not, just continue with your story," the Marquis answered. "Tell him I have been

20

pressed by my family, which is true, to produce an heir, and I have at last decided that is what I shall do, and the announcement will be in the '*Gazette*' in three days' time."

"In three days?" Lady Burnham exclaimed. "But suppose it is – not?"

"It will be!" the Marquis said firmly. "What you have to do is persuade your husband to wait for three days. Point out to him that if he starts a divorce case and then my engagement is made public, people will not only question his evidence, but will suspect he is being deliberately spiteful because my horses have beaten his in the last two races in which we both had runners."

Lady Burnham drew in her breath and clasped her hands together.

"That might – convince George – it might," she said. "You know he thinks that the sun rises and falls on his horses."

The Marquis was well aware of this, knowing that the reason why Lord Burnham was so frequently away from home was that he was attending race-meetings in various parts of the country.

"Keep on impressing upon him," he continued, "that he will be considered by his friends exceedingly unsporting if he ruins the happiness of a young girl who has just become engaged to me."

"I will tell him! Of course I will tell him that!" Lady Burnham said eagerly, "and – Quintus, I think it is very – clever of you. It is the one – argument George might listen to."

"That is what I thought," the Marquis said with just a faint tone of satisfaction in his voice.

He looked down at Lady Burnham for a long moment, then he lifted her hand to his lips.

"Goodbye, Leone,' he said. "Thank you for the happiness you have given me. I am only sorry that I should have been instrumental in bringing you so much distress."

"I love you – Quintus!" Leone Burnham replied, "and I

21

know I shall never – love anybody – again as I love – you!"

She gave a little sob before she went on bravely:

"But if George were successful, and we became – married, we would only – grow to hate one – another."

"We can only hope and pray," the Marquis said, "that is something which will never happen."

He kissed her hand again before he added:

"Go now. Do exactly what I say, and make no attempt to communicate with me."

"No, of course not," she answered, "and thank you – dearest Quintus, for – everything – but most of all for being – you."

She rose as she spoke, pulled the dark cape she was wearing close around her and looked up for one long moment into the Marquis's eyes.

Then she turned without another word and walked away. A moment later he heard the Chapel door close behind her.

The Marquis sat down again in the pew.

He knew it would be wise to wait for quite some time before he left the Church just in case Leone was being watched and he had anyhow, a great deal to think about.

What was more, he was well aware that his thoughts had to be translated into action which must be made public in three days' time!

. . . .

Two hours later the Marquis set out from Stowe House driving his most spectacular team in a travelling Phaeton which had only recently been delivered.

It was one of the fastest vehicles the coach-makers had ever built, and he had spent a great deal of time suggesting improvements in its design which had undoubtedly added to its speed and comfort.

Looking exceedingly elegant with his tall hat slightly on the side of his dark head, his Hessian boots gleaming like polished ebony, and his cravat tied in the style which was both the envy and despair of the Dandies, he and his entourage drew the eye of everybody either walking or riding in Park Lane.

As the Marquis turned his horses North he thought with satisfaction that the groom who had gone ahead of him over one-and-a-half hours ago would reach Dawlish Castle within four hours.

This would give the Duke plenty of time to prepare for an unexpected, but certainly welcome guest.

It was in the Chapel that a conversation he had had two months ago with the Duke of Dawlish, had come to him like a flash of light in the darkness of despair.

They had been talking together after a race-meeting which they had both attended the previous day and the Marquis had said casually:

"Have you added any more horses to your stable this season, Your Grace?"

"Unfortunately no," the Duke replied. "My trainer tried to tempt me with a couple of yearlings which he says have great promise, but the fact is, Stowe, I cannot afford to expend a great deal of money on horses at the moment."

The Marquis had looked surprised, but before he could say anything the Duke went on:

"I have a daughter coming out this Season. That means a Ball in London, with an astronomical number of bills from dressmakers, milliners, and God knows what other shop-keepers."

The Duke had sighed before he continued:

"It is a case of gowns or horses and you can guess which, as a married man, I have to choose!"

The Marquis had laughed and the Duke, who had a sense of humour, also laughed before he went on:

"If you take my advice, Stowe, you will remain a bachelor for as long as you can! They will catch you in the end, but you might as well give them a good run for their money!"

The Marquis had laughed again.

"I will, Your Grace. You can be sure of that!"

The Marquis knew that the Duke would welcome him without question, as a son-in-law!

The Duchess who had already married off two of her daughters, would accept him as her third without querying any conditions he might impose as to the immediacy of the announcement.

It would be, the Marquis thought, quite an advantageous marriage if he had to make one, from his point of view.

God knows he had no wish to be married.

He had expected to enjoy his bachelorhood for at least another five to ten years before there was any real need for him to settle down and produce an heir.

But if he had to be 'leg-shackled' as the servants called it, then it might as well be to a girl whose interests would almost certainly include an appreciation of horse-flesh.

The Duke of Dawlish was an acknowledged sportsman and almost as popular with the racing crowd as he was himself.

As the Marquis drove his horses through the traffic with an expertise which proclaimed him a Corinthian, he was trying to remember if he had ever heard the name of the Duke's third daughter, or set eyes on her.

He supposed she must have been at some of the race-meetings at which her father was always present.

He could remember the Duchess looking dowdy but aristocratic, and their older daughter Mary, who had married the Viscount Cannington, a chinless young man, heir to an Earldom, but he did not recall the rest of the family.

She would however the Marquis told himself, because she was her father's daughter, make him the type of wife that he was expected to have and she would know how to play hostess at his family seat in Buckinghamshire and at Stowe House in London.

Up to now when the Marquis gave a house party he

always enlisted the assistance of his mother whose beauty and wit had been proverbial until she had to retire from social life owing to being almost crippled with rheumatism.

At other times her chaperonage had not been requested, and as he drove on, the Marquis thought of the very amusing bachelor parties he had given that would now unfortunately come to an end.

At these parties, because most of the male guests were bachelors, the females were the most alluring 'bits o' muslin' who were the toast of St. James's or actresses for whom the Bucks and Beaux waited at the stage-door night after night at Drury Lane or the Italian Opera House.

"They were great fun!" the Marquis thought nostalgically.

He decided that marriage or no marriage, his house in Chelsea would still contain an occupant about whom his wife would remain in complete ignorance.

Once they reached the open road and there was little traffic, the Marquis drove his team hard.

He reckoned that even allowing an hour for luncheon at a Posting Inn which the groom on his way to Dawlish Castle would have notified of his intended arrival, he should reach his destination at the comfortable hour of four o'clock.

That would give him time to make the acquaintance of his future bride, and inform the Duke of his intentions.

He would send a groom back to London first thing in the morning so that his secretary could insert the notice in the '*Gazette*' in time to greet the eye of Lord Burnham when he opened his newspaper on Wednesday morning.

He could not imagine there would be any hitch in his plan, unless of course, Leone could not persuade her husband to wait the three days he had requested.

The Marquis who liked being prepared for every contingency, was thinking that he still had a day in hand in case, although it was unlikely, the Duke's third daughter might already be engaged.

This was such an outside chance that it really did not warrant much consideration. Yet the Marquis was used to taking no chances where his plans were concerned.

He also faced the truth that if the worst came to the worst and Burnham went ahead, he had no wish whatsoever to be married to Leone.

He thought she was one of the most beautiful women he had ever seen, and he had not been surprised when she had surrendered herself to him because he had never had the experience, when he desired and pursued a woman, of being rebuffed.

Although he admitted that their love-affair had been at times ecstatic, the Marquis, if he was honest, now knew that while it had been enjoyable, it was something which he had no wish to continue for the rest of his life.

In fact the idea of such a thing happening appalled him.

He drove on, and now he asked himself why his love-affairs always ended so quickly and invariably in his becoming satiated and bored with the woman in question, however lovely she might be.

It would be impossible, he thought, to find anybody more beautiful than Leone. She was also sweet and gentle and had given him, as usually happened, unreservedly her whole heart.

The Marquis always wondered a little cynically what was wrong with other men that their wives invariably seemed unawakened to the rhapsody and fire of love.

He could never remember making a woman his without her telling him that never in her life before had she been so aroused that the love he gave her, or rather she gave him, was very different from what she had enjoyed with her husband.

'It must be that I am a very good lover,' he thought complacently, as he drove on.

He knew it was another accomplishment of which he could be proud.

Thinking it over he supposed he had a pride in himself and in his achievements ever since he had been a small boy.

It was his father who had said to him:

26

"The world is there for you to walk on and do not forget it! Be a fighter and a conqueror, a man who achieves what he desires, and forget all this damned nonsense about being a 'miserable sinner' as they teach you in Church!"

The old Marquis had laughed as he had added:

"If I did not think myself better than most of the people with whom I associate, I would blow a piece of lead through my head!"

His son had laughed too at the time, but he had also thought how magnificent his father looked!

He lived it was true almost like a King on his estate which was run in such an exemplary fashion that it was the envy of and an example to all their neighbours.

He had thought then that he would like to emulate his father, and it was something he had tried to do.

When he had inherited and grown older he felt as if every day he became prouder of what he possessed and of what he himself had achieved.

"Pride comes before a fall, Stowe! And don't you forget it!" one of his contemporaries with whom he was having an argument once shouted at him.

The Marquis had not deigned to reply, but he thought now that he had come very close to falling. In fact he was standing on the edge of a precipice, and only his intelligence and a bit of luck could save him.

Without thinking he pushed his horses a little faster, as if he was determined to get to Dawlish Castle with all speed and save himself before he should drop into complete disaster.

After quite an edible luncheon at the Posting Inn, and having drunk half a bottle of his own claret so that he felt in a slightly more mellow mood, the Marquis continued his journey.

There was now less then two hours' drive before he reached the Castle, and he was planning what he would say to the Duke on arrival to explain his unexpected visit and also what he would say when he asked the Duke's daughter

27

to honour him by becoming his wife.

'I suppose girls are romantic,' the Marquis thought, 'and she will expect me to be flattering, and of course, persuasive.'

When he thought about it he realised he did not even know any young girls, and as far as he could remember, he had never talked with one, except to say 'How do you do', or 'goodbye'.

He had certainly never danced with one because he had made it a rule, unless it was completely unavoidable, never to dance at Balls.

In fact he invariably ended up at the card-tables unless he visited a dance-hall with his friends to appraise the pretty Cyprians.

"I wonder," the Marquis said to himself, "what young girls talk about? And what are their interests?"

He knew only too well what interested them once they had the ring on their finger and after a year or two had presented their husband with an heir.

In an extraordinary manner they developed the art of flirtation and became amusing and witty, which was certainly not an accomplishment they were taught in the School-Room.

As the Marquis thought back over conversations he had had with Leone and a number of other lovely women before her, he felt there was, if he was truthful, very little originality in what they said.

They certainly laughed at his jokes, appeared to blush at his compliments, then enticed, allured and invited him with every word that was spoken, with every glance of their eyes, with every movement of their bodies.

He enjoyed it, of course he enjoyed it. He would not be human if he did not like being wooed.

But it was all very obvious and as he thought back it had really become somewhat monotonous! That was the reason why, however beautiful the ladies were, his love for them if that was what it was, never lasted very long.

Just in the same way, the occupants of his very comfortable, well-furnished little house in Chelsea changed so often.

"What am I looking for?" the Marquis asked himself.

The question surprised him, but he did not know the answer.

He drove round a curve in the road, then pulled in his horses sharply.

"There's an accident, M'Lord," the groom sitting behind him announced unnecessarily.

"I can see that!" the Marquis said.

He brought his team to a walk, then moved gradually forward.

Accidents on the road were quite usual, and this looked no different from those he had encountered before.

It was quite obvious that a Stage-Coach, an overloaded cumbersome affair, had come into collision with a cart driven by a yokel who had doubtless been asleep, his horse left to plod uncontrolled in the middle of the road.

The accident could only just have happened for the horses were still plunging wildly, while the coach was at a dangerous angle with two wheels in the ditch and both the luggage and the passengers sliding off the open roof.

"Go and see what you can do, Ben," the Marquis said to his groom.

"Very good, M'Lord, but you knows as well as I do I'm not as good at it as Your Lordship," Ben replied.

It was an impertinence, but the Marquis accepted it as the truth.

"Very well," he said, "hold the reins while I sort it out."

Ben obeyed him and the Marquis descended from the Phaeton and walked towards the accident.

The noise was almost deafening. The coachman, red in the face, was yelling at the yokel who had been driving the cart and was now yelling back.

Meanwhile the horses belonging to the stage-coach were still plunging with the shafts up round their necks, while a crate of hens had broken open and the birds were cuckling about all over the road.

As the shouting of the two drivers and the violence of their language was increasing, the Marquis reached them.

"Go to the heads of your horses, you fools!" he commanded in a voice which reduced the two men to silence.

Then as they turned to look at him they recognised authority when they saw it and hurriedly obeyed.

Some farm labourers had by now, appeared from nowhere and several men had alighted from the coach. On the Marquis's orders, given crisply and in a manner which made it impossible for him not to be obeyed, they righted the coach.

The women passengers who, on his instructions, had climbed out to make the load lighter, stood by complaining tearfully of the shock they had suffered.

The cart which had caused the trouble had been pulled onto the verge, the stage-coach horses had quietened down and the passengers were once again reluctantly getting back inside the coach, when the Marquis was aware that a very pretty young girl was looking at him admiringly.

She was plainly but tastefully dressed and he thought from her appearance that she was a Lady.

At the same time there was no doubt that she was making no effort to get back into the coach, but was just looking up at him wide-eyed, with an expression which the Marquis could not help feeling was very flattering.

"You can continue your journey now," he said, and because he thought it would please her, he raised his tall hat.

"You were wonderful! Wonderful!" she exclaimed. "I thought when we almost overturned I would be crushed to death!"

"I am glad you have been saved from such an unpleasant fate," the Marquis replied.

"By you!"

As she spoke the guard of the stage-coach shouted:

"All aboard! Or we'll leave without ye!"

It was obvious he was speaking to the girl, as everybody else had resumed their seats.

"They are waiting for you," the Marquis said.

The girl turned her head.

"I will walk, thank you," she said in a clear, youthful and, as the Marquis noticed, educated voice.

"Do you live near here?" he enquired.

He looked around as he spoke in surprise and could see no sign of any houses.

"It is only a little over a mile," the girl replied, "and I have no wish to listen to the whining and complaining there will be from the other passengers."

"I can understand that," the Marquis said, "so may I suggest as I am travelling in the same direction that I give you a lift in my Phaeton?"

He saw the expression of delight in her eyes before she exclaimed:

"May I really come with you? It would be very exciting!"

The Marquis smiled and walked to where his horses were waiting.

He helped the girl into the seat beside the driver, then went round to the other side of the vehicle to take the reins from Ben.

As they drove off he realised she was looking at him in a rapt manner as if she could hardly believe what she saw.

"Do you always travel by coach?" he asked.

"Yes, every day," the girl replied. "My teacher lives in the next village from ours and it is the easiest way for me to reach her."

"And what does she teach you?" the Marquis asked.

"French. She was an *emigrée* years ago, and she has, Papa says, a perfect Parisian accent."

The Marquis looked surprised.

"Your father is a good judge of French?"

"Papa is an expert on languages of all sorts, but especially French, Italian, Greek, and of course Latin."

She saw the astonishment in the Marquis's eyes and laughed.

"Does that sound strange to you?"

"It does rather," the Marquis admitted, "because I would not expect to find a language scholar in the middle of such rural surroundings."

"No, I suppose not, but Papa writes books. Rather dull and very erudite."

"Which means, I suppose, that you do not read them?"

"Not if I can help it, but my sister reads them and encourages Papa to keep writing even though it makes very little money."

The Marquis smiled at the ingenuousness of it and at that moment saw ahead of him the cottages of a small village and the tower of a grey stone Church.

"Is this where your home is?"

"Yes," his passenger replied. "It is next to the Church. You will see the gateway and, please, drive in through it. I do want my family to be impressed by your horses and of course, by you!"

The Marquis laughed and when they reached the gateway he drove in even though it required quite a feat of skilful driving.

It was only a short distance to the front door of a low, attractive house which because it was adjacent to the Church-yard he felt must be the Vicarage.

He was just about to say goodbye to his passenger, when as he drew his horses to a standstill she alighted with the swiftness of a bird in flight and ran in through the open front door.

He could hear her shouting:

"Ajanta, Ajanta, come quickly! Darice, come and see how I have been driven home!"

Because he felt amused by the commotion he was causing, the Marquis attached his reins to the running-board, noted that Ben was already at the horses' heads and stepped down.

As he walked through the front door into a small oak-panelled hall, he heard a voice in the distance say:

"What are you talking about, Charis?"

"I have been rescued – rescued from a terrible accident by the most exciting man with superb horses! And a Phaeton which is smarter than anything you have ever seen before! Oh, Ajanta, do come and meet him!"

There was a pause before the Marquis heard the same voice say:

"What do you mean. .rescued? The last time it was a bull you were saved from, and the time before that it was a ghost."

"This time it was an accident!"

The Marquis waited, then he heard footsteps coming towards him and a moment later the girl who had been his passenger appeared pulling by the hand another taller and very much lovelier edition of herself.

He had thought the girl to whom he had given a lift was exceedingly pretty, but he was for the moment spellbound by the beauty of her older sister.

She was wearing an apron and he thought she must have been cooking, but nothing could disguise the gold of her hair, the vivid, almost startling blue of her eyes, and a fair skin which made him think of the petals of a flower.

The Marquis fancied himself as a connoisseur of beauty as of everything else that was good in life.

He knew as he faced the young woman who was called Ajanta that he had never seen in London, Paris or anywhere else anybody so lovely.

He had taken off his hat on entering the house and now standing with it in his hand he waited with a faint smile on his lips for what he thought would be the introduction.

But before the girl to whom he had given a lift could speak Ajanta said:

"I understand from my sister that she had been involved in an accident from which you rescued her."

"The Stage-Coach collided with a cart," the Marquis

explained. "There was a great deal of commotion, but I do not think anybody was injured."

"He sorted it all out as if he was a magician!" Charis enthused. "Then he brought me home in his Phaeton. Come and look at it, Ajanta!"

She pulled on her sister's hand as she spoke, but Ajanta did not move.

"First I must thank the gentleman who has rescued you," she said. "Thank you, Sir. It was very kind of you to bring my sister home. She has a propensity for getting into situations from which she has to be rescued."

"So I heard you say," the Marquis smiled. "But this incident, I assure you, was not as formidable as being chased by a bull."

"Charis was not chased," Ajanta replied. "She merely thought she might have been, but luckily there was a student passing who brought her home safely."

There was no doubt that Ajanta was amused that her sister had been what she thought of as 'saved' and the Marquis said:

"I am glad that she is so lucky, or perhaps, as you think, resourceful."

Ajanta gave him a little smile as if she appreciated the subtlety of her sister's adventures, then she said:

"I am sure, Sir, that you wish to be on your way, and we can only thank you for your kindness."

"On his way?" Charis echoed. "That is very inhospitable of you, Ajanta. Surely it would be polite to invite the gentleman to have luncheon with us?"

The Marquis saw the amusement in Ajanta's eyes vanish and he was surprised when she said stiffly:

"I think, Charis, you should thank this gentleman for his kindness, then go and wash your hands."

"Of course I want to thank you," Charis said to the Marquis. "But I am sure as it is luncheon time you would like to have something to eat before you travel any further."

The Marquis was just about to refuse and say that he had

already had luncheon when he saw the expression on Ajanta's face and it surprised him.

She was so lovely that he thought it was almost his right that she should admire him and be impressed with him in the same manner as her sister was.

And yet this country girl was, although he could hardly believe it, looking at him in an uninterested manner, and was clearly anxious for him to leave as quickly as possible.

Because it piqued him, he replied:

"It is kind of you, and although I am not hungry, I would be very grateful, after all the dust of the road, if I could have a drink."

"Of course you can," Charis cried triumphantly. "What would you like?"

"It is a question of what we have," Ajanta said coolly. "I am afraid, Sir, it is a choice between lemonade or cider."

She spoke as if she was quite certain he would refuse both but the Marquis said:

"I should be delighted to accept a glass of cider, if it is not giving you too much trouble."

He thought for a moment Ajanta would say it was but instead in a tone which was almost defiant, she replied:

"I will fetch it for you. Charis will show you into the Dining-Room."

"I will," Charis agreed.

She pulled off her unfashionable bonnet as she spoke and the Marquis saw that her hair was fair and very long, not as gold as her sister's, but still exceedingly pretty.

He wondered who could possibly have sired such beautiful children and thought it would be amusing to meet their father.

Then as if his thought communicated itself to Ajanta he heard her say to somebody in the distance:

"Go and tell Papa that luncheon is ready, and tell him to come at once or he will be late for the Funeral he is taking this afternoon."

As she spoke there was the sound of feet running down a

passage and a moment later another girl, very much smaller, but exceedingly pretty came into the room.

She stopped for a moment to look at the Marquis, then ran on.

"That was Darice," Charis explained. "Come into the Dining-Room. You are sure you are not hungry?"

"Quite sure, thank you. I will be very content with the cider your sister is bringing me."

The Dining-Room was a square room with a large oval table in the centre of it, covered, the Marquis noticed, with a linen cloth that was spotlessly clean.

The table was laid for four people. Charis brought up a chair and put it beside the one at the top of the table.

"You had better sit next to Papa," she said, "and I will sit next to you, because I want to talk to you. But if Papa starts on his pet subject I shall never get a word in."

"I cannot believe you are ever silent for long," the Marquis teased.

Charis laughed, and as she did so her fair hair which reached down to her waist rippled as if with little golden waves.

The Marquis was looking at her when Ajanta came into the room carrying a stone jug in one hand and a large dish in the other.

The Marquis took the stone jug from her knowing it would contain the home-brewed cider which many farmers made specially for their workmen.

As he set it down on the sideboard, Ajanta put the dish she was carrying on the table and left the room.

Charis fetched a tumbler and as the Marquis poured himself out some cider Darice came back holding the hand of a man who looked, the Marquis thought, exactly as he might have expected the father of such exceptionally beautiful children to look.

The Vicar when he was young must have been amazingly handsome, and even now with his hair turning white and lines on his face, he was an outstandingly good-looking man.

"How do you do, Sir," he said to the Marquis. "I hear from my youngest daughter that you have rescued Charis from some unfortunate occurrence."

"An accident with the Stage-Coach, Papa," Charis said before the Marquis could reply.

"Oh, dear, not another one!" the Vicar exclaimed. "They travel far too fast down these narrow lanes. I have said so a dozen times."

"I agree with you," the Marquis said, "but I was fortunately able to put things right, and your daughter is none the worse."

"I am glad about that. May I know your name?"

"Stowe," the Marquis replied.

He was so used when he said his name to a look first of surprised recognition, then of admiration, that it was unexpected when the Vicar said:

"I am very grateful to you Mr. Stowe, and I hope you will join us for luncheon. My name is Tiverton."

As he spoke Ajanta had come back into the room carrying a pile of plates.

"We have already asked Mr. Stowe, Papa, if he will join us for luncheon," she said, "but he says he only wants a glass of cider."

"That seems very inhospitable," the Vicar said. "I wish I had something stronger to offer you, but I am afraid I cannot afford a good claret. When it comes to alcohol, I dislike anything but the best."

The Marquis smiled.

"I agree with you, and I am very content with cider which I am sure is locally brewed."

"From our own apples. I find. . ."

"Please, Papa, sit down," Ajanta interrupted. "As you know, luncheon is late today because we were waiting for Charis, but you must not be late for the Funeral."

"Funeral?" her father questioned. "Have I a Funeral this afternoon?"

37

"You know you have, Papa, for Mrs. Jarvis. You cannot forget it."

"No, I must not do that," the Vicar agreed as he seated himself in his chair at the top of the table.

As the Marquis sat beside him he was certain from the way he spoke that forgetting Funerals and other Services was something the Vicar was prone to do.

"I understand, Sir," he said politely, "that you write books."

An eager expression came into the Vicar's face.

"I am at the most interesting part of the one I am writing now, and it is exceedingly annoying to be called away."

"What is it about?" the Marquis enquired.

"I am compiling all the Religions of the World. It is a very interesting subject, very interesting indeed! And this will be my sixth, no, – seventh volume!"

"When Papa was writing about the Greeks I was christened Charis," a voice beside the Marquis interposed.

"And your sister?"

The Marquis looked at Ajanta as he spoke and because she had her back to the window she seemed to have a halo of light round her golden hair.

He thought she looked like a Greek goddess but for the moment he could not place the name.

"Ajanta was born when Papa was writing about the Indian religions," Charis informed him. "Darice when he was doing the Persian, and Lyle when he was writing about Catholicism in France."

"You have certainly set yourself a formidable task, Sir," the Marquis said to the Vicar.

"It is very interesting, Mr. Stowe, I assure you."

"And does your son wish to follow in your footsteps?"

"No, indeed," the Vicar replied. "Lyle is at Oxford at the moment, and I am afraid his tastes are not very erudite, in fact as his reports tell me, not at all scholarly."

"I am sure Lyle will do very well when he has been there a little longer," Ajanta said.

The way she spoke which was obviously in defence of her brother made the Marquis aware that he meant a great deal to her.

She started to serve the food she had prepared for her family seated round the table.

The Marquis was aware that it was rabbit stew, and from the aroma of it, well cooked with herbs, onions and fresh mushrooms.

Although he had already eaten too much to want any more, he almost regretted that he could not taste it.

He however sipped his cider and was amused by this homely scene around him.

Then he was aware that Darice was looking at him as admiringly as Charis had and he thought that she was exactly like a small pink and white Boucher angel.

He smiled across the table at her and she asked:

"Are you very, very rich?"

"That is not the sort of question you should ask," Ajanta corrected sharply.

"Why not?" the Marquis enquired just to be argumentative and to Darice he said:

"What makes you think I am rich?"

"Because you have four horses, and horses are very, very expensive to buy and keep."

The Marquis laughed.

"That is true enough, as I know to my cost."

"I am afraid," the Vicar said, "all my family want to ride, but as we can only afford one horse for riding and one to take me in a gig round the Parish, they have to take it in turns."

"And Darice cheats!" Charis informed him, "because she makes Ajanta give up her turn to her."

Darice looked across the table at her sister before she said quietly, looking the Marquis thought, more than ever like a small angel:

"That is not only an unkind thing to say, but sneaky!"

"Darice is right," Ajanta said, "and we have no wish to

bore Mr. Stowe with our family problems."

"But I am interested," the Marquis protested.

He spoke as if he was challenging Ajanta, and she looked down the table at him in a manner which made him think she accepted his challenge as she replied coldly:

"I cannot imagine why."

"Very well, I will tell you why," the Marquis replied. "I have never in my life, though I have travelled a great deal and met a great many people, ever encountered a family of three young women who are so astoundingly and breathtakingly beautiful as you are!"

As he was speaking directly to Ajanta he saw first a look of astonishment in her eyes, then one which he could only interpret as disapproval.

She did not however get a chance to speak because Charis gave a cry of pleasure.

"Do you mean that?" she asked. "Do you really mean we are prettier than anybody you have ever seen before?"

"That is what I said," the Marquis answered.

"I told you that you are wonderful!" Charis said, "and now I think you are the nicest man I have ever met!"

"That is enough, Charis!" Ajanta said sharply.

As she spoke she rose from her place at the end of the table, picked up her plate and Darice's, and put them on the sideboard.

Then she carried out the dish which had contained the rabbit without looking at the Marquis.

He had the feeling that as she left there was a flounce of her cotton skirts which amused him.

CHAPTER TWO

By the end of luncheon the Vicar was regaling the Marquis with an extremely interesting account of the book he was writing on the Moslem religion.

"I only wish there was somewhere near here where I could find the reference books I require," he said. "I would like to pay a visit to Oxford, but I am afraid. . ."

Before he could go any further Ajanta interrupted:

"That is something, Papa we cannot. . ."

She stopped.

As if she was suddenly aware that the Marquis, a stranger, was listening to their private affairs she said in a somewhat repressive tone:

"We will speak about it later, Papa."

"Yes, of course," he agreed as if he realised he had been indiscreet.

Ajanta turned to Charis.

"Hurry up, Charis," she said. "You know you have a great deal of homework to do before Mrs. Jameson comes to you at five o'clock."

As she spoke Ajanta removed the remains of the treacle pudding from the table and put it on the sideboard.

She then looked at her father who she knew was longing to continue his conversation on what was at the moment the subject that absorbed him to the exclusion of all else:

"Papa," she said. "I think you should be getting ready for the Funeral. They will expect you to be at the Church gate to meet them when the coffin arrives."

"Yes, of course. You are quite right, my dear," the Vicar agreed.

He rose from the table and as the Marquis rose too he held out his hand.

"I am very pleased to have met you, Mr. Stowe. I only wish we could continue our most interesting conversation. It is not often I meet anybody these days who knows anything about the East and their extremely complex religions."

"I too have enjoyed our talk," the Marquis replied.

Ajanta was already leaving the Dining-Room pulling the reluctant Charis with her, who was looking back over her shoulder at the Marquis.

When they reached the Hall she managed to free herself from her sister's grasp and going to the Marquis's side she said:

"You have some magnificent horses, Mr. Stowe!"

"I thought you would appreciate them," the Marquis replied with a smile.

Charis hesitated for a moment. Then she said in a somewhat lowered voice:

"I have written a poem about a horse. Would you like to have it?"

"That is very kind of you."

He realised as he spoke that Ajanta was frowning at this interchange and it amused him to annoy her.

Charis made a little sound of delight and started to run up the stairs as quickly as she could.

The moment she was out of hearing Ajanta said to the Marquis with a sharp note in her voice:

"Please, Mr. Stowe, do not encourage Charis. She is only sixteen and imagines herself to be in love with every man she meets."

"Is that such a distressing thing to happen?" the Marquis enquired.

"It is to us," Ajanta replied simply. "When Charis is infatuated with some stranger she has met by chance, she will moon about for days, paying no attention to her lessons which is hard on the rest of the family who have to pay for them."

She spoke with a note of acidity in her tone and clearly resented what she thought was a mocking smile on the Marquis's face.

He however noted that her blue eyes seemed to flash at him in a way that he had never seen before.

"I appreciate your problem, Miss Tiverton," he said, "and therefore I will say goodbye immediately, and thank you for a delicious glass of cider."

He held out his hand as he spoke, but Ajanta appeared not to see it as she was moving towards the front door as if to speed his departure.

He was following her when there was a cry from the stairs and Charis came running down towards them.

Ajanta turned at the front door and now she held out her hand.

"Goodbye, Mr. Stowe," she said, "and I do hope your wife will soon be better. You must be very worried about her."

Both the Marquis and Ajanta were aware as she spoke that Charis had stopped halfway down the staircase.

For a moment she seemed indecisive as to whether she should go forward or retreat the way she had come.

Then she quickly dropped the piece of paper she had been holding and came down the last steps into the Hall without it.

The Marquis looked at her enquiringly and she said:

"I could not – find the – poem."

Without waiting for his reply she went through the front door and outside to where Darice was already patting the horses and telling Ben how magnificent they were.

"First round to you, Miss Tiverton!" the Marquis said to Ajanta as he passed her.

He climbed into the driver's seat and as he picked up the reins Ben ran to jump up behind.

"Goodbye! Goodbye!"

43

The two younger girls stood waving as the horses went down the drive.

When the Marquis had manipulated his team through the narrow gateway he looked back to see that there was only Darice standing on the steps watching him go.

He was smiling as he drove on, thinking it had been an amusing incident in what otherwise had been a disastrous day.

He would never see the Tivertons again, but he could not help thinking that the beauty of the three daughters of an obscure country Parson was something unique which he would remember.

But now his own problems enveloped him like a dark cloud, and he drove his horses as fast as possible because he was in a hurry to reach Dawlish Castle.

. . . .

Sitting in the large, draughty, rather ugly Dining-Room the Marquis was aware that his plans so far had been upset in a way he had certainly not expected.

He had planned that when he arrived at the Castle he would speak to the Duke immediately.

He would tell him he had decided it was time he married, and in view of their long acquaintanceship on the race-course and in their Clubs he could not imagine anything more suitable than that their families, both of great importance in the history of England, should be united by marriage.

He had planned his words with care, and he was certain that the Duke would be delighted at his suggestion, and not only because he was so wealthy.

It was as well to like one's in-laws, the Marquis thought, otherwise he could imagine hours of boredom when he would have to entertain them at Stowe Hall and perhaps attend family festivities at Dawlish Castle.

His plans however had been upset when on arrival he was shown into the Library to find to his surprise that the

Duke was not alone, but had three of his closest friends with him.

As the Duke held out his hand with a smile of greeting, Harry Strensham, whom the Marquis had seen only two days previously in White's exclaimed:

"Dammit, Quintus! We tried to keep the Sale from you, and I swear it was not I who let the cat out of the bag!"

"I am not guilty," another friend exclaimed. "I have not seen Quintus for a week!"

"I have been deliberately avoiding him!" the third announced.

"What is all this about?" the Marquis asked.

"Now, come on, Quintus! You need not play the innocent with us," Harry laughed. "You have obviously heard about the Trevellyan Sale, and we were hoping because he is such a greenhorn he had omitted to invite you."

As his friend spoke the Marquis understood exactly what he was talking about.

When Lord Trevellyan had died it was rumoured that his son, who was living abroad, might be thinking of selling up his stable.

The Marquis had however heard nothing about a Sale, and as nobody had mentioned it to him he assumed that the new heir would carry on racing the horses on which his father had spent so much time and money.

However, because the new Lord Trevellyan had no knowledge of horse-flesh and was not interested in the 'Sport of Kings' he had arranged to have a private Sale.

The Marquis's friends had thought because he did not mention it that he had not been invited and they knew they had a better chance of obtaining bargains than if he was bidding against them.

It was just part of his usual luck where horse-flesh was concerned, the Marquis thought, that quite by accident he had stumbled on a plot to exclude him which would in fact, if he had not had more important things on his mind, have annoyed him considerably.

Lord Trevellyan's stable contained some very fine animals which he would be glad to add to his own and now he had learned what was going on, he had every intention of taking advantage of the fact.

"I must say, I think it was extremely underhand of all of you," he said when, with his usual quickness of mind, he had grasped the situation.

"All is fair when it comes to women and horses!" Harry laughed. "As you have beaten us to the post far too often where both are concerned, we believed that for once we had a sporting chance."

"I will make you pay for this, Harry!" the Marquis said good-humouredly.

"I thought it unlikely that you of all people, Stowe, would not have your ear to the ground, when it concerns anything to do with racing," the Duke said. "So as soon as I got your note I knew quite well why you wanted to come here today."

"Is no one else joining us?" the Marquis asked.

"Only Eddie," Harry replied, "and we have all agreed that as he is so hard up we will let him have one horse without bidding against him."

"I am certainly prepared to concede that," the Marquis said. "But I shall run you up quite considerably, Harry, for the way you have treated me! You are supposed to be my friend."

"I am," Harry replied, "but your purse is a great deal longer than mine, as you well know!"

They all laughed and until it was time to dress for dinner the conversation was exclusively about horses and their merits.

Now sitting on the Duchess's right with Lady Sarah, the remaining unmarried daughter, on his other side, the Marquis found himself thinking how incredibly dull the dinner would have been if it had not been that three of his friends were fellow guests.

The Duchess could talk of nothing but the iniquities of her neighbours who had not contributed to the restoration of an ancient Abbey which she considered an historic monument.

She droned on in a monotonous voice which made it impossible for the Marquis to concentrate on what she was saying.

On his other side Lady Sarah in contrast had apparently nothing at all to say.

He had had a shock when he first saw her.

Because the Duke was quite a fine-looking man, he had somehow expected that his daughter, if not a beauty, would certainly be pleasant to look at.

But Lady Sarah was plain, dumpy and had, as far as the Marquis could see, nothing to recommend her except that she did not ramble on like her mother.

Because he was determined to make an effort where she was concerned, as soon as the Duchess began to bore Harry who was on her right with her complaints, he said to Lady Sarah:

"Are you coming with us to the Sale tomorrow?"

"No," she replied. "I do not like horses!"

The Marquis was astonished.

"What do you mean – you do not like horses?" he asked, thinking it was something no woman had ever said to him before.

Even those who were not keen riders and had no wish to hunt always expressed an interest in the horses which the Marquis rode, and those he raced.

"I am frightened of them," Lady Sarah admitted.

"What do you do with yourself when you are in the country?" the Marquis asked. "Your father has a good shoot here. Does that interest you?"

"I think shooting is cruel!" she replied, "and I hate the noise!"

"Then what do you do every day?" the Marquis persisted.

47

"I do not know really," Lady Sarah said helplessly. "There always seem to be things to do with Mama."

The Marquis thought this was very heavy going and rather like riding through thick mud.

"Are you a great reader?" he enquired. "Your father certainly has a very fine Library."

"I do not have much time for reading," Lady Sarah replied.

The Marquis looked at her and came to the conclusion that she really was one of the most unprepossessing young women he had ever seen.

She had a sallow complexion, her hair was mousy with a touch of red in it, and her eye-lashes were the same colour, which made him think of a ferret.

He suddenly had a vision of Ajanta's golden hair and her dark blue eyes sparkling with anger because she did not want him in the Vicarage.

The way she had behaved constituted a challenge because it was very unusual for the Marquis not to be warmly welcomed wherever he went, and anybody who entertained him tried to delay his departure rather than hasten it.

He decided to make another effort with Lady Sarah, and he said:

"What do you do when you are in London? I can quite understand you prefer living there where you have Balls to go to and lots of other parties."

"I do not like Balls," Lady Sarah replied. "I have had dancing lessons, but I find it difficult to follow the way the gentlemen in London dance."

She spoke in a languid manner and the Marquis was aware that here was another subject that did not interest her.

They sat in silence and the Duchess seized the opportunity to regale him once again with the iniquity of those who did not wish to preserve ancient landmarks.

Suddenly he told himself that this was something he

could not endure for the rest of his life.

He could already see the years stretching ahead of him with the Duchess's voice droning on and on, and Lady Sarah, looking dull and frumpish at the end of his table, boring the unfortunate men who must sit on each side of her.

"I cannot do it!" the Marquis said beneath his breath, then remembered the alternative.

His chin went up and he thought that anything, even Lady Sarah, was better than the ignominy of being co-respondent in a divorce case brought by his most bitter enemy.

"I will speak to the Duke after dinner," he told himself.

But the opportunity did not arise.

Immediately after dinner they all sat down to play cards and when finally the Marquis rose from the table the better off by several hundred pounds, it was to find his host had slipped away without him being aware of it.

"Where is the Duke?" he asked Harry.

"His Grace is determined to have a clear head for the Sale tomorrow. He has admitted that he cannot spend much money and he is not going to waste what little he can afford on some animal who has gone in the wind!"

The Marquis laughed.

"I am quite certain Trevellyan will have nothing like that in his stable."

"You can never be sure at these sort of Sales," Harry said. "Remember we are not dealing with Trevellyan who was always as straight as a die, but his son, a ne'er do well from all I hear, and quite capable of pulling a fast one over on us."

"Then we certainly must be careful," the Marquis agreed.

Only when he had reached his bedroom and was undressing with the help of Ben who when the Marquis did not travel in style acted as valet, that an idea came to him.

It suddenly struck him that he had been rather stupid in

thinking that being married was the only way he could save himself.

The idea was right, but while the announcement of his engagement might spike Burnham's guns and prevent him from going ahead with his case, there would be no need, if he was really crafty, actually to reach the altar!

How could he find himself tied for life to a dull dowd like Lady Sarah?

While he was thinking he walked to the window to stand looking out blindly into the night while Ben, not having been dismissed, fidgeted about the room while he waited for his orders to retire.

Finally the Marquis made up his mind.

"Call me at six o'clock tomorrow morning, Ben," he said. "I want to ride Rufus, and tell Jim to come with me on the horse that brought him here from London."

Jim was the groom who had ridden ahead with the Marquis's letter to the Duke inviting himself to stay.

"Very good, M'Lord," Ben said. "I understands from what I 'ears downstairs that Your Lordship'll be attending the Sale."

"That does not start until noon," the Marquis said. "I will be back for breakfast and will drive over to Lord Trevellyan's house in the Phaeton."

"Very good, M'Lord."

Ben picked up the Marquis's evening-clothes and moved towards the door.

"Good-night, M'Lord."

The Marquis did not hear him. He was still deep in thought.

It was nearly an hour later before he finally got into bed and by then he had everything planned.

His last thought before going to sleep was that he had been, even for him, unusually clever.

He could certainly celebrate his intelligence by buying all the best horses obtainable at the Sale tomorrow whatever they might cost.

. . . .

Ajanta, on her knees scrubbing the floor, was humming a little tune.

It was a lovely day and she was planning that if she had the time she would go and look at the bluebells in the wood.

She knew there was just one week in every year when the wood behind the Vicarage was a carpet of blue which she secretly thought was very much the colour of her own eyes.

It was a very lovely sight and her mother had said once:

"The beauty of the bluebells when I see them in the spring remains with me all through the year, and when I am feeling depressed or worried, which is not often, I think of them, and they lift my heart so that I am laughing again."

"You are very poetical, Mama," Ajanta had teased her.

"Could I be anything else when I have your Papa and of course the four most adorable children in the world?" her mother replied.

"I will go and look at the bluebells," Ajanta promised herself, "and they will make me forget the bills that are coming in at the end of the month and the riding-boots that Lyle needs so badly."

She worried over Lyle even more than her father.

"Look after Papa," had been her mother's last words to her before she died.

But her father could manage when he was writing to slip away into a world of his own which helped him to forget for a little while the heart-break and misery he felt at his wife's death.

Lyle was different. He was young and so good-looking and he not only worked hard, but wanted to enjoy himself with his friends at Oxford.

But it was almost impossible to find the money for his fees, the clothes he wanted and pocket money, which small though it was was essential if he was to have any fun at all.

"If only I could make some money," Ajanta was thinking.

But what opportunities were there in a small village consisting of fewer than two hundred people?

Nevertheless because the sun was shining and because she would see the bluebells later in the afternoon she went on humming.

Suddenly just ahead of her brush on the flagged floor there appeared almost as if by magic two black shining objects which she identified as highly polished Hessians.

She looked up, gave a little exclamation of surprise and sat back on her heels.

Standing in the kitchen, looking exceedingly elegant and overwhelmingly proud and handsome, was the man who she considered had forced his way into the house only yesterday.

If Ajanta was surprised, so was the Marquis.

He had rung the bell and when it was not answered he thought it not unlikely that it was broken.

He had therefore walked in through the open front door expecting to find somebody at home of whom he could enquire the whereabouts of the Vicar.

There was nobody in the Sitting-Room which he thought, although it was small and the carpet threadbare, had a definite charm about it.

There was nobody in the Study which was filled with books from floor to ceiling while books also were piled on every table and chair and even on the floor.

The Marquis therefore decided that the only chance of receiving the information he wanted was to find a servant.

He walked past the Dining-Room in what he was sure was the direction of the kitchen and was just about to address the woman he saw scrubbing the floor when the glinting gold of her hair told him it was Ajanta.

As she looked up at him he thought she was even lovelier than he remembered.

He forgot for the moment what he had intended to say and merely asked:

"Do you have to do this? Surely there is somebody who could do it for you?"

52

"Of course," Ajanta replied. "At least half-a-dozen women in the village would be delighted to have the job, but they would also expect payment."

Then as if she thought it was rather undignified to reveal their poverty to a stranger she said in a different tone, and there was an undoubted note of aggression in it:

"What do you want? Why are you here?"

"I want to see your father."

"He is away for the day and will not be back until late this afternoon."

The Marquis's lips tightened for a moment before he said:

"In which case, I would like to talk to you, Miss Tiverton."

"What about?" Ajanta enquired. "As you can see, I am very busy."

"What I have to say is not only of great importance, but it is urgent, and incidentally it closely concerns you."

"It concerns me?" Ajanta enquired. "I cannot imagine how anything that you wish to say to my father, Mr. Stowe, can possibly concern me."

The Marquis smiled and it made him seem more human and certainly more attractive.

"Most young women would not expect me to speak of anything but themselves."

Ajanta however was not listening. She was looking down at the floor.

She only had half the kitchen to finish and she was debating whether it would be possible to ask Mr. Stowe to wait until she had completed the scrubbing.

Then she thought he might stay and watch her and that would be embarrassing.

"I hope you will not be very long," she said as she rose to her feet. "I have a great deal of cleaning to do, and I also have to prepare the luncheon."

The Marquis did not reply.

He merely watched her as she took off an apron made of

sacking which she wore over a plain gown made of cheap cotton which he suspected she had made herself.

It however, did not disguise the grace of her figure, the smallness of her waist, or that she had slim hips and undoubtedly, the Marquis thought, long athletic legs.

It struck him he had been right when he first saw her that she might have been a young Grecian goddess, and a Greek name would have been more appropriate than one that came from India.

Without hurrying Ajanta pulled down her sleeves which she had rolled up above the elbows and buttoned them neatly at her wrists.

Having placed the bucket and scrubbing-brush against the wall of the kitchen she said:

"Perhaps you will come into the Drawing-Room, but please do not keep me long, otherwise I shall have no time this afternoon to see the bluebells."

As she spoke she realised she had been following her train of thought and had not meant to mention anything so personal to this importunate stranger.

The Marquis was immediately curious.

"Bluebells?"

"In the woods at the back of the garden," Ajanta explained, "but it can be of no interest to you."

The Marquis did not reply to this, he merely followed Ajanta as she walked back along the passage and opened the door of the Sitting-Room which he had already visited.

He realised now as he looked at it that some of its charm was due to the masses of flowers which stood on every table.

They seemed to bring in the sunshine and the gold of the daffodils certainly echoed the gold of Ajanta's hair.

As she stood by the fireplace and raised her blue eyes to his, he thought he could understand why she wanted to see the bluebells.

"Well, what is it, Mr. Stowe?" she asked. "I do beg of

54

you, if you have problems, not to worry my father unless it is absolutely necessary."

She had a sudden fear as she spoke that perhaps Mr. Stowe had come to try and interest her father in a charity or obtain money from him in one way or another.

Then she told herself having seen the horses he drove and the manner in which he was dressed that such an idea was ridiculous.

"What is. .it you. .want?" she asked again, and there was an undoubted note of apprehension in her voice.

"Suppose you sit down?" the Marquis said.

He spoke with an air of authority which made Ajanta obey him without argument.

As she sat in the nearest armchair which faced the window the Marquis took her place in front of the mantelpiece and remained standing.

"When I came here yesterday," he said, "I realised from the things you said and the remarks made by your father that you are finding it difficult to make ends meet."

He saw Ajanta stiffen and thought she was about to say that it was none of his business. Quickly he went on:

"I understood you are finding it hard to pay your brother's fees at Oxford and you told me that it was a mistake for your sister to waste the money you paid her teachers."

"And to waste time mooning about over you," Ajanta added as if she could not help saying what she was thinking.

"Has she been doing that?"

"Of course she has! At that age girls are always wildly over-romantic and Charis is no exception."

"But you did not suffer in the same way?" the Marquis enquired.

"I do not think this is what you came here to talk about to Papa."

"It certainly indirectly concerns it," the Marquis replied, "and as I see you are impatient, Miss Tiverton, I will continue."

"Please do."

"What I am telling you," he said, "is that I need your help in a very difficult and personal problem, and if you will give it to me, I am prepared to pay you the sum of £2,000 for your services."

If he had dropped a bomb at her feet Ajanta could not have been more surprised.

For a moment she could only stare at the Marquis, until when she could speak she asked:

"Is. .this a. .joke?"

"No, of course not," the Marquis replied. "I am deadly serious, and perhaps it is better, now that I think about it, that I should make the offer to you rather than to your father. I have a feeling, although I may be wrong, that he is unworldly and money does not at all concern him."

"That is true," Ajanta conceded. "But why should you want to offer us, whom you have only just met, such an enormous sum of money, and what can we possibly do to earn it?"

"The person who earns it will be you, Miss Tiverton."

"Me? How?"

"That is what I am going to explain to you, and let me say in case you still doubt my intentions, that this is entirely serious and an absolutely sincere plea for help."

"You. .did say. .£2,000?" Ajanta asked in a very low voice.

As she spoke the Marquis thought that her eyes were very revealing and he could see she was thinking what this could mean to them all.

He had the idea, although he could not be sure, that the last thing Ajanta would consider would be help in the house so that she did not have to scrub the kitchen-floor.

He chose his words with care before he replied:

"I am in a position whereby it is imperative for me to become engaged to be married within the next three days. I say 'engaged' and it will be an engagement which may have to last three, four, perhaps six months. After that it can be terminated and there will be no question of my actually being married to the person to whom I become affianced."

Ajanta stared at him incredulously and he went on:

"That is why I need your help for which I am prepared to pay the sum of £1,000 now once the engagement has been announced, and a further £1,000 when it comes to an end. Then we part amicably with the explanation that we have jointly decided that we are not compatible."

"I think you must be mad!" Ajanta ejaculated.

"I am asking, Miss Tiverton, for your help."

Ajanta did not look at him.

"The answer is 'no'! The whole idea is preposterous! I am sure Papa would be extremely shocked at my pretending that I wish to be married when I was aware all the time that it was something which would never happen."

There was a slight pause, then she added with dignity:

"I think, Mr. Stowe, you should leave. I have listened to your proposition and refused it. There is no point in our discussing it any further."

"I quite understand," the Marquis replied in a cold voice. "I made a mistake. I thought when I came here yesterday that you loved your family and would wish to do your best for them. Now I see I was wrong and I can only offer my apologies."

As he spoke he took a step as if he would walk towards the door.

"I *do* love my family!" Ajanta cried as he finished speaking. "I love them and would do anything for them, but. . ."

". . .help them by earning £2,000," the Marquis concluded. "If that is love, it is a very selfish emotion."

"How dare you say such things to me!" Ajanta answered. "I look after Papa and the girls. . ."

"And deny your brother," the Marquis interrupted, "the horses he could ride, the sports he would enjoy and all the other pleasures one can have at Oxford."

"Lyle is very happy at Oxford," she said angrily.

57

"But he needs money," the Marquis replied. "I was there myself, and I know just how much everything costs."

Ajanta walked to the window to stand with her back to him.

He knew she was seeking a way of escape as he had sought last night, and the answer had come to him like a star shining in a dark sky.

Now looking at Ajanta's hair gleaming with gold from the sun he waited with a smile on his lips, confident that he would get his own way.

"How. .could anybody. .believe that. .you would. . suddenly want to. .marry. .me in such a. .headlong. . manner?" Ajanta asked at length, and it seemed as if the words were being dragged from her lips one by one.

"If you look in the mirror you will realise that most people will not be surprised," the Marquis answered.

As he spoke in a dry, almost impersonal voice, it did not sound particularly a compliment.

Ajanta turned round.

"I am. .sure Papa will not. .believe it."

"Then you must be clever and convince him – unless you intend to tell him the truth, which I am sure would be a mistake – that it was love at first sight."

"That is what. .he felt for. .Mama."

She spoke hardly above a whisper, but the Marquis heard.

"Which makes it easier," he said. "I met you yesterday at luncheon-time, and knew you were the one person I had been seeking all my life."

He spoke in a mocking tone of voice.

"Such things do happen!" Ajanta said sharply, "and you are not to laugh about it."

"I will certainly not laugh if you will agree to do what I want," the Marquis replied. "In fact I will be very, very grateful."

"I do not. .really see. .how I can do. .such a. .thing," Ajanta said helplessly.

"You will do it because you sensibly and wisely realise what a difference this money will make to your family in the future," the Marquis said. "And I am doing it because it will save me from a very uncomfortable situation I do not wish to discuss."

"And you do not. .think it is. .wrong of. .me?" Ajanta asked.

Now she was no longer aggressive, but somehow seemed only young and afraid and, the Marquis thought, because her eyes had softened, very beautiful.

"I always consider it wrong," he answered, "to refuse the gifts the gods offer, in whatever form they come. Most people call it luck, but perhaps your father would think of it as manna from Heaven."

"That is what I am. .trying to. .tell myself it. .is," Ajanta murmured. "At the same time I cannot help. .feeling that I am doing. .something that is not only. .reprehensible, but. .frightening."

"There is no need to be frightened," the Marquis said. "I will look after you and all you have to do is to agree that the announcement should appear in the '*London Gazette*' tomorrow."

"Tomorrow?" Ajanta echoed. "But that is far too soon!"

"Not for me."

"But what about your family, if you have one?"

"I can deal with my own family," the Marquis replied. "All you have to do is to deal with yours."

"I do not know. .what to. .say to Papa."

The Marquis smiled.

"I feel that you will manage him as competently as you manage your sisters. May I assume that you will help me from this moment, and not try to back out?"

"If I give my word I will not break it," Ajanta said with a touch of pride.

"Then shall we say it is a deal?" the Marquis asked. "Let us shake hands on it."

He put out his hand as he spoke but Ajanta looked at him apprehensively.

"I am. .frightened," she said. "I am making a. .leap in the dark and I am not. .certain where I shall. .end up."

"I promise you it will be in a very soft place."

He saw a faint smile curve her lips and she replied:

"It might be a thorn bush or a bed of thistles."

He laughed.

"I promise you it will be neither. In fact, if it is a bed it will be one filled with goose-feathers."

Ajanta gave a little laugh as if she could not help it and put her hand in his.

The Marquis's fingers as they closed over hers were very strong and in some way she could not quite understand reassuring.

Then he released her and said:

"Will you allow me to write a note which my groom will then take to London?"

"Yes, of course," Ajanta said, "and I think it would be easier if you wrote at Papa's desk because everything in the way of pens and paper is there in his Study."

"Thank you."

He let Ajanta lead the way although he had already seen the Study in his tour of the house.

He sat down at the desk and once again she went to the window almost as if she needed the air coming through the open casement.

"Now I just have to get this correct for the '*London Gazette*'," he said, "and by the way, I have omitted to tell you until now, but my name is actually the Marquis of Stowe!"

Ajanta looked at him in astonishment.

"The. .Marquis of Stowe!" she exclaimed. "Then your horse won the Derby last year."

"Yes, '*Golden Glory*'."

"Lyle was quite certain he would win, and we were all so pleased when he did."

"I shall enjoy showing him to you."

There was silence, then Ajanta said in a hesitating voice:

"Are you. .suggesting that I should. .visit you at your. .house?"

The Marquis who was inspecting the quill pens which were lying on the desk looked up to say:

"But of course! I shall want to take you to London and to my family seat in Buckinghamshire."

"But. .how can. .I come with. .you?" Ajanta asked. "I have Charis and. .Darice to consider."

"I shall be delighted for you to bring them with you," the Marquis answered, "and I was thinking that as Stowe Hall is only about ten miles from Oxford your father might wish to seize the opportunity while you are there to do the research he was talking about yesterday."

"I see you have thought of everything," Ajanta said, "except that your family and your friends, if they meet me will not think I am a very. .suitable bride for you. In fact, I doubt whether when they. .see me they will believe the engagement is a genuine one."

For a moment the Marquis looked surprised. Then his eyes twinkled.

"Like all women," he said, "you are thinking of clothes. It is the first time I have known you to be really feminine, Ajanta."

"Of course I am thinking about my clothes," she retorted sharply. "It may be part of your plan that I should look like a beggar-maid the noble Marquis has picked up in the gutter but it is not a role I particularly wish to play."

The Marquis laughed.

"You are not giving me credit for my really rather outstanding gift of organisation," he said. "Of course you shall have the right gowns. I realise they are essential, and some of them will be waiting for you when you reach London. That is another note I have to write now."

"I have no wish to expend the money you will give me on such frivolities," Ajanta said quickly.

"It will not be your money you spend," the Marquis replied, "but mine."

Ajanta stared at him. Then she said:

"That is something I cannot allow! Mama would not approve!"

The Marquis squared his chin and she knew he intended to be obstinate.

Before he could speak however she added:

"I have my pride, My Lord, and I also know what is right and. .conventional."

"I also know," the Marquis retorted, "that it would be extremely stupid and short-sighted, in fact, quite idiotic for you to pay for clothes with money which you know full well is required by your brother and sisters for their education!"

Ajanta made a little sound of protest, but before she could speak, he went on:

'Even £2,000 will not last for ever, and if you do not need it later for your trousseau, Charis will certainly want to look romantic and glamorous, and so in a few years will Darice."

He saw by the expression in her face that he had partially convinced her and he said:

"You really must allow me to conduct this campaign in my own way. I have appointed myself Commander and I cannot have a constant mutiny on my hands. I expect to be obeyed without question!"

"That is not being a Commander, but a tyrant!" Ajanta flashed.

"In an emergency one has to take the law into one's own hands," the Marquis said loftily, "and that, Ajanta, is what I am doing."

He spoke clearly and rather louder as he added:

"Regardless of social conventions and what is done or not done by a lot of old Dowagers, I intend to provide you with the clothes you need, just as if I were producing a Play at Drury Lane or a Ballet at Covent Garden where I would dress my actors and actresses for their parts. Is that understood?"

There was a pause before Ajanta said in a low voice:

"I. .I suppose I. .must agree."

"It would be very foolish if you did not. Now let me get this down so that there can be no mistakes."

He read aloud as he wrote:

"The engagement of marriage is announced between the Marquis of Stowe and Ajanta, daughter of the Reverend Maurice Tiverton and the late Mrs. Tiverton."

He looked across the room at Ajanta as he asked:

"Is that correct?"

There was just a slight pause before she answered:

"Y.yes."

The Marquis folded the piece of paper on which he had been writing and took another sheet and put it on the blotter in front of him.

"Now," he said, "I suggest you go upstairs and find a dress which fits you exactly. My groom will take it to a dressmaker with whom I have had dealings before and whose taste I can trust, who will provide you with several gowns which you can wear immediately."

Ajanta's eyes seemed very large in her face as she looked at the Marquis.

He had a feeling that once again she was going to protest, to argue with him.

Then as her eyes met his he said quietly:

"While you are upstairs I am going to write a cheque for £980, because as I think you have quite a number of expenses before you leave home, and perhaps some small purchases to make, I will give you £20 which I have with me in notes and gold."

Ajanta drew in her breath.

· Then as if she felt the Marquis overpowered her and it was impossible to go on fighting, impossible to do anything but obey him, she walked swiftly across the room and left the Study closing the door behind her.

CHAPTER THREE

Driving back to Dawlish Castle the Marquis thought with satisfaction that he had been exceedingly clever.

Everything had gone according to plan except that he had had a considerable battle with Ajanta to get his own way.

Even when she had come downstairs with the gown to be used as a pattern tied up in a neat parcel, she was still fighting him.

He thought that she was very pale, but her skin had the translucence of a pearl as she stood in the doorway of the Library.

While she was upstairs he had been writing several letters that must go to London, and he put down the quill pen and waited for her to speak.

"You are quite. .certain," she asked in a low voice, "that this is the. .right thing for me to. .do?"

"It is what I want you to do," the Marquis said, "and quite frankly I think you would be very foolish to refuse me."

He thought of another argument as he spoke and added:

"It is not only the money, which I am well aware you need, but also most young women would find it a considerable advantage to be engaged even for a short while to the Marquis of Stowe."

He was saying what was in his mind and he was not prepared for the flash of fire which came into Ajanta's blue eyes.

"What you are really saying, My Lord," she said, "is that I should be on my knees, thanking you for condescending to anybody so unimportant, who in any other circumstances would certainly be beneath your notice."

"I have not said that," the Marquis retorted.

"But you are thinking it," Ajanta said. "So let me make it quite clear that I am not impressed by your social importance or by your title, My Lord. I am doing this entirely so that I can help Lyle at Oxford and give my sisters a better education than we can afford at the moment."

She paused and the Marquis said with a mocking smile:

"And of course you must not forget your father and yourself."

"I have certainly not forgotten Papa!" Ajanta replied aggressively. "As you have already pointed out, he will be able to go to Oxford for the research which he needs for the new book."

"I shall return to London first thing tomorrow morning," the Marquis said, "and there make arrangements for you all to be brought to Stowe Hall in Buckinghamshire. Your father will accompany you."

There was silence. Then Ajanta said in a different tone of voice:

"I suppose it would not be. .possible. .although we are. .officially engaged. .for me to. .stay here? It will be. .very embarrassing for me to meet your family and friends. .if that is what you. .intend."

"It will not be embarrassing if you play your role properly," the Marquis said. "My family will be overjoyed that I am to be married and will do everything in their power to welcome you."

"And what will they. .feel when our. .engagement is. . terminated?'

"I will deal with that when the time arrives," the Marquis said. "All you have to do, Ajanta, is to be charming, look lovely, and of course, make them believe you have some affection for me."

There was no doubt of the sarcasm in his voice, but he did not expect the answer that Ajanta gave him.

She looked at him for a long moment before she said:

"I do not know what sort of trouble you are in or why you need my help, but I can only hope that the reason is not a dishonourable one."

"Why should you think it might be?" the Marquis asked.

"Why else, when the most noble Marquis of Stowe has the whole social world to choose from, should he seek the assistance of an obscure Vicar's daughter?"

"The answer is quite simple," the Marquis retorted. "You are an extremely intelligent and beautiful young woman."

Ajanta looked at him in surprise and he saw the colour rise in her cheeks before she turned away with what was obviously a little flounce to place the parcel she carried down on a chair near the door.

The Marquis addressed the letter he had written to his secretary, then another to:

"Lady Burnham,
Park House,
Park Street,
London"

What he had written was, he thought, a very clever letter which even George Burnham might find convincing.

"My dear Lady Burnham,
I have taken your advice, and I want you to be the first to know that Ajanta Tiverton has accepted my proposal of marriage.
We are very happy and it is all due to your kind advice for which I am very grateful.
Ajanta is coming to stay at Stowe House for a few

days after which I shall hope to bring her to London to make your acquaintance.

Again my most grateful thanks.

I remain,
Yours sincerely,
Stowe."

Thinking it over to himself as he rode back through the fields towards Dawlish Castle, the Marquis thought George Burnham would have difficulty reading anything into the letter other than what it said.

'Damn it, he must be convinced!' he thought.

At the same time he knew that Burnham was like a bull-dog, and once he got his teeth into an idea it would be hard to make him give it up.

Having sent Jim off to London with the parcel containing Ajanta's gown, a letter to his secretary with the announcement to the '*Gazette*' and the letter to Lady Burnham, he said goodbye to Ajanta saying:

"I will send my travelling-chariot for you all the day after tomorrow. It will be accompanied by a brake for your luggage, but you will not need very much as the new clothes I have ordered from London will be awaiting you."

He spoke in the commanding voice he always used when he was giving orders, and he thought it would prevent her protesting any further and ensure that she carried out his plans exactly according to his wishes.

She did not speak for a moment. Then she said:

"What am I to say to Papa?"

"Tell him I came here to ask formally for his permission to pay my addresses to you, but as he was away from home and I had a pressing engagement I, unfortunately, could not wait to see him. But I will of course discuss everything with him when he arrives at Stowe Hall."

He was aware that Ajanta was going to say that her father would think this very odd and he added:

"I should not tell him when the engagement is to be announced. I cannot believe you take the '*Gazette*' and it will not appear in '*The Times*' until Friday or Saturday."

Ajanta did not reply and the Marquis said quickly:

"Goodbye, Ajanta. Try to think of this as an adventure – something which your family will enjoy, even if you are determined not to do so."

His words because they were provocative made her eyes flash at him again, and he swung himself onto his horse and rode off.

He did not look back, being sure if he did so that Ajanta would not be waiting to see him out of sight.

At least, he thought, as he neared Dawlish Castle, skirmishing with Ajanta would be considerably more interesting than trying to talk as if through a thick fog to Lady Sarah.

When the Marquis reached the Castle he found he had taken longer than he had expected at the Vicarage, and when he entered the Breakfast Room there was only Harry there.

He looked up as the Marquis entered.

"It is unlike you to be so late, Quintus," he said. "I thought you never overslept."

"I have been riding," the Marquis replied.

He went to the sideboard to help himself to a rather unappetising dish of eggs and bacon, but there was nothing else he fancied.

"If you had told me you were going I would have come with you," Harry said. "There is something I wish to tell you when we have the chance to be alone."

The Marquis looked at him sharply.

There was something in the way Harry spoke which made him guess what the information would be, and he was aware that his friend was choosing his words with care.

Because he thought it would be embarrassing if Harry warned him that Burnham was on the warpath he said:

"Actually I have news for you which I think will surprise you."

"What is it?" Harry asked.

"I am engaged to be married!"

Harry stared across the table as if he could not believe his ears.

"You are what?" he finally asked.

"It will be in the '*Gazette*' tomorrow morning," the Marquis said, "and I hope, as one of my oldest friends, you will give me your good wishes."

"Good God!" Harry exclaimed. "There is one thing about you, Quintus, you always spring a surprise when one least expects it! I had no idea you were contemplating matrimony after what you have said so often about that particular state."

The Marquis smiled.

"That was before I met Ajanta."

"Ajanta?" Harry questioned. "Have I met her?"

"No, you have not. Her name is Ajanta Tiverton, and need I say, she is very beautiful."

"I wonder why you have never introduced me to her?"

"I am too wise for that," the Marquis replied. "You might have attempted to steal a march on me as you were doing over the Sale today."

"Good Heavens! I would never try to rival you in the field of love!" Harry said. "You know as well as I do that where women are concerned you pass the winning-post before the rest of us have left the start."

The Marquis smiled.

"You are very humble all of a sudden."

"Tell me about this beauty who has captured you when so many others have failed," Harry asked.

"I am not going to say anything until you have seen her for yourself," the Marquis replied. "And, Harry, I would rather you did not tell the others until after I have left here. Their curiosity and their congratulations would be equally embarrassing."

70

"Of course they will be curious and so am I," Harry said. "You are the most avowed bachelor in the whole of St. James's and I had thought your interest recently lay in a very different direction."

"When one wants to keep something secret," the Marquis said lightly, "it is always wise to get people looking in the wrong direction."

"So that is what you have been doing!" Harry said. "Well, all I can say, Quintus, is that you have deceived both me and a large number of other people, including one who is in a dangerous mood."

The Marquis knew that he was referring to George Burnham and he managed to reply again as if it was a matter of no great importance:

"If ever a man was a fool who cannot see directly what lay under his nose and is always ready to fly off at a tangent, it is Burnham!"

Harry looked at him quizzically but he said no more, and the Marquis deciding he had had enough breakfast rose to his feet.

"Come and have a look at the Duke's stable before we leave," he said. "I have just decided that I cannot face the food in this place any longer, and will start back to London the moment the Sale is over, or I have bought everything that takes my fancy."

"That means we may get some of the animals you reject at a reasonable price," Harry said.

"Tell me what you want particularly," the Marquis replied, "and you know I will not bid against you."

"That is very decent of you, Quintus," Harry smiled. "There are in fact two horses I particularly want as long as they have not deteriorated since I last saw them."

. . . .

When the Marquis had left, Ajanta sat down on a chair in the hall as if her legs would no longer support her.

She found it impossible to believe that what had

71

happened was true, rather than part of some mad dream from which she would wake at any moment to find herself upstairs in her small bed.

Then she walked back into the Library to find lying on the desk where he had left it a cheque made out in her name for £980, besides two notes of £5 each, and ten golden sovereigns.

Ajanta had never seen so much money in the whole of her life and it struck her that perhaps it was fairy-gold and when she touched it with her fingers it would vanish.

She picked it up and it was still there, then she put it down again so that she could fold the cheque carefully.

She then decided that she would not tell her father of the transaction she and the Marquis had made together. In fact, nobody must know.

She was ashamed of it, she thought it degrading.

At the same time, some part of her brain was already busy deciding what she would buy, and knowing what an enormous difference the money was going to make to their lives.

Lyle could have the riding-boots he wanted and some really smart clothes such as he had never had, and he could have a horse of his own in the vacations.

He would also be able to afford to hunt as he had always wanted, not with the 'hobbledehoy' farmers' pack, but the one in which the members' fees had until now, been too high.

Then she thought of Charis and decided the best thing for her would be to go to a Young Ladies' Seminary for a year.

She knew her mother had attended one, and she had often spoken of how different her lessons had been there from jogging along with one Governess at home.

"When I married your father," she had said, "if I had not been better educated than most young women of my generation, I should never have been able to share his interests or help him with his work as I have done."

72

She sighed before she said:

"Oh, dearest, I do wish we could afford to send you to a good School, even for a few months."

"I am sure, you and Papa have taught me just as much as I could have learned at any School," Ajanta had replied loyally, but she knew her mother was unconvinced.

Yes, she decided now, Charis must go to School, and it would do her a great deal of good.

She would stop mooning about after men and instead enjoy the company of other girls of her own age, and the competition it would entail.

'Charis should be surrounded by young people,' Ajanta thought, 'and the same will apply to Darice, when she is a little older.'

She had often thought because they were all so intelligent and quick-witted that their brains were stagnating, lacking the stimulus that was so important.

'The money will enable me to do so much for Charis and Darice,' Ajanta thought.

Then she remembered what she had to do and felt apprehensive.

She was too intelligent not to realise that the Marquis had manipulated her very cleverly in getting her to agree to his preposterous proposal.

'He is clever, and he knows it,' she thought, 'and he is also proud and very conceited.'

She knew the idea of a mock engagement was something he would never have thought of suggesting to a girl he considered to be one of his own class.

'For instance, he would never dare to suggest it to Lady Sarah,' Ajanta thought.

She had seen Lady Sarah on one or two occasions when she had attended some County function or been asked to the garden-party that the Duke and Duchess gave every third year, and to which they invited practically everybody in the County.

It was a condescension on their part, as Ajanta knew,

but their guests included the local Parsons, the Doctors, and even the more important Yeoman Farmers who lived on the Estate.

"When the Duchess speaks to me," Ajanta said to her mother after the last one they had attended, "she always makes me feel as if I am a charity child and I should be thanking both God and the Duke for my bowl of gruel!"

Her mother had laughed.

"I know exactly what you mean, dearest. I always think of the Duke and Duchess when I sing:

> " 'The rich man in his Castle,
> The poor man at his gate,
> God made them high and lowly
> And order'd their estate.' "

"Oh, Mama, I wish I could say that to them," Ajanta laughed.

"If you did," her mother replied, "I am quite sure they would take it seriously and not think it in the least funny."

Something Ajanta missed desperately when her mother had died was having somebody to laugh with.

The Vicarage had always seemed to be filled with laughter, but for a long time after her death it appeared as if her husband would never smile again.

It was Ajanta who realised that the gloom engendered by his sense of loss was bad both for Charis and Darice, and she forced herself to make jokes and to inveigle her father into seeing the funny side of things.

It was a tremendous effort because she knew in losing her mother life could never be the same again.

It was Lyle more than anybody else who helped to create a more or less normal atmosphere which Ajanta knew her mother would have wanted, even though they could never forget her.

Lyle came home full of enthusiasm about how wonderful Oxford was, how many new friends he had, what pranks they played when they were not working.

He found it hard to adjust himself to ride alone because there was only one horse, and to have no friends to invite to meals. But he was always happy with Ajanta who because she loved him was prepared to listen for hours on end while he talked about himself.

She knew that Lyle would be the easiest member of the family where her unexpected engagement was concerned.

He would be exclusively interested in the prospect of riding the Marquis's horses, the attempt to copy the way he tied his cravat, and the invitation to visit Stowe Hall.

Ajanta thought now she had been very obtuse when the Marquis had said his name was Stowe not to realise that he must be one of the great race-horse owners about whom Lyle talked continually.

She was sure now that Lyle must have told her about him after his horse had won the Derby.

'It was stupid of me, Stowe being an unusual name, not to guess that he was the owner of "*Golden Glory*",' she thought. 'But one would hardly expect a stranger who rescued Charis to be a Marquis!'

She then remembered she had not only to tell Charis of her engagement, but also to explain away her misleading reference to Mr. Stowe's 'wife'.

"The whole thing is becoming more and more complicated!" she said crossly.

At the same time, as she carried the cheque, the notes and the sovereigns upstairs to her bedroom to hide them in a drawer in her dressing-table, she was planning how tomorrow she would drive, if her father did not want the gig, to the small market-town, that was only two miles away.

There she would deposit the cheque in her father's Bank.

One blessing was that because the Vicar was so engrossed in his books and so forgetful of everything else he had arranged that she could sign cheques on his account.

"It is very unusual, Vicar," the Manager had protested.

But because he admired anyone who could write a book, he finally agreed.

She knew that the Manager who was used to their having only a very small amount of credit in their account, and sometimes being overdrawn, would be astonished.

She told herself the only explanation she could make was that she had been left a legacy by one of the Marquis's relations.

"A Godmother would sound convincing," she said, then thought it was another falsehood.

"Lies! Lies! Lies!" she exclaimed to herself. "It is what I have to do, but it is wrong. It is something I should not do, not only as myself, but as my father's daughter."

She paused, then she said slowly and distinctly:

"I hate him! I wish he had never come into my life!"

At the same time irrepressibly her heart was singing because Lyle could have his fun, Charis could go to School, and she would no longer have to teach Darice herself, but could employ the teacher for her whom Charis would no longer require.

. . . .

Driving in the exceedingly comfortable travelling-chariot which the Marquis had sent for them made Ajanta feel as if she was leaving behind one world for another.

It was strange to see such an impressive vehicle outside their door, and to realise the six horses pulling it were of such superior breeding that she could only stare at them spellbound.

The servants in their smart livery seemed to have stepped straight out of a fairy-story.

Ever since the Marquis had left them everything that happened seemed unreal, not as in a dream, but as if she was being propelled by some supernatural force and could hardly draw her breath, let alone think.

When she told her father rather hesitantly that she was engaged to the Marquis, he had said:

76

"I thought him an extremely intelligent man, but I had no idea that you had met him before yesterday."

Ajanta drew in her breath.

"It was actually the first time, Papa, but he said that he fell in love with me as you did with Mama the moment you saw her."

"That is true," the Vicar said. "I had never seen anybody so beautiful, and I felt she must have stepped out of Heaven itself."

Ajanta knew that her father and mother had met when he had just left Oxford, and when they looked into each other's eyes everything else in the whole world had paled into insignificance.

"That is how I want it to be," she told herself.

She had felt resentful because she was missing something precious and she thought the Marquis was encouraging Charis to think herself in love with him.

'I expect he has that effect on every woman he meets,' she thought scornfully, 'but it is certainly something that will not happen to me.'

"I am looking forward to visiting Stowe Hall," her father was saying.

"Yes, Papa, and the Marquis suggested it would be a good opportunity for you to go to Oxford from there and get on with your research."

"He is very kind and thoughtful," the Vicar said. "I am finding it very difficult to get the detailed information I require for Chapter Four in which I describe Mecca and what it means to those who can wear the green turban."

The way her father spoke told Ajanta that he was already thinking of his writing.

She therefore left him in his Study and walked down to the village to ask the elderly retained Clergyman who lived in the house at the far end if he would be kind enough to take any Services that were required until her father returned.

"I knew it would not be long before your father felt the

urge to go to Oxford again," the old man said jovially, "and you must encourage him, Ajanta, to finish this next volume of his work. I enjoyed the last one on Zen Buddhism more than I can say."

"Papa will be delighted that it pleased you," Ajanta said.

"A brilliant man, your father! Brilliant! And of course I will do anything in my power to fill in for him while he is away."

"Thank you! You are very kind," Ajanta said and hurried back to the Vicarage to set off for the market-town.

Once she had paid in her cheque she could buy things for Charis and Darice, although the choice in such a small place was limited.

However the new ribbons for her chip-straw bonnet sent Charis into ecstasies of delight, and the blue sash to go round a plain muslin gown that Ajanta had made for her younger sister made Darice look more than ever like a small angel.

Ajanta had always thought that Darice looked as though she had stepped straight out of an allegorical painting, and she would have been irritated if she had known that the Marquis thought the same thing.

In spite of every resolution to be grateful she could not help resenting the way he swept them off their feet and forced them to carry out his instructions without even an apology for causing such inconvenience.

"If he thinks I am going to go down on my knees and thank him for everything he does," Ajanta told herself, "he will be mistaken. He is doing this entirely for his own selfish ends."

At the same time it was exciting to travel faster than she had ever travelled in her life before in a carriage that was so well sprung and so well cushioned that the roads might have been as smooth as a table.

Their leather trunks, all now old and worn looked extremely incongruous, Ajanta thought, when they were put into the smart brake which being drawn by only four

78

horses left an hour-and-a-half before the chariot.

The servants with the two vehicles had stopped the night at a Posting Inn which was only about half-an-hour's drive away from the village.

"His Lordship wishes us to get to Stowe Hall as quickly as possible, Miss," the Coachman explained, "and the horses are raring to go, so you'll not find the journey too tedious."

They stopped for what they all decided was a delicious luncheon the meal having already been ordered by the servants on the brake that had stopped there earlier.

The manner in which they were received by the landlord, the comfort of the private parlour into which they were shown, and the bottle of the very best claret which had been ordered for the Vicar, with lemonade for the girls, made everybody but Ajanta almost hysterical with praise for their host.

"How can he think of every detail?" Charis asked.

She had been fulsome in admiration of the Marquis and was undoubtedly once again in love with him now she had learned he was unmarried.

She had said to Ajanta this morning:

"I think it extremely unfair that you should marry him. I found him first, and if it had not been for me he would never have come to the Vicarage."

"I know, dearest," Ajanta replied. "But he is really too old for you. In another year or so you will undoubtedly meet a young man of the right age."

"I cannot believe there could be anybody as good as the Marquis!" Charis said petulantly. "But you are prettier than I am, and I suppose it was only to be expected that he would like you best."

It was with difficulty that Ajanta did not reply:

"I do not like him in the slightest, and he is only making use of me!"

Then she told herself she must not even think such things, because they were so close to each other as a family that they could often read one another thoughts.

Although she had done her best to make her two sisters look smart for the journey, Ajanta had not bothered about herself.

It was in fact, a very long time since she had had a new gown, and she thought a little ruefully that the one in which she must travel and which had once been a pretty shade of blue was now both worn and faded.

There was nothing she could do about it, except hope that the Marquis's relatives would not notice and that he really meant it when he said clothes would be waiting for her at Stowe Hall.

She thought it was because of her appearance that he had not kept to his original plan to take her first to London.

She would not look quite so out of place in the country to which she was used, but she was quite certain in London her appearance would evoke the scorn and contempt of the Marquis's smart friends.

"They might be suspicious," she told herself, "that he should wish to marry anything so dowdy and out of place."

She was well aware that if he had not been so strong, so masculine, so broad-shouldered, he might have been described as a 'Dandy'.

Lyle had explained in great detail what Dandies wore, the elegance of their clothes, the way their Hessian boots polished with champagne shone so that one could see one's face in them, and the height of their cravats.

She had thought Dandies were rather feminine, foolish creatures, but she could certainly apply neither of those adjectives to the Marquis.

After such a good luncheon and the excellent claret the Vicar fell asleep in his corner of the carriage, and so did Darice.

Charis on the other hand had no wish to miss anything, and she chattered away asking questions for which Ajanta had no answers, until finally she said:

"Oh, do be quiet for a little while, Charis! I have a

80

headache. I wish like Papa I could sleep."

"I expect really you are feeling over-excited because you are going to see the person you love," Charis said romantically.

"It is not that at all," Ajanta said without thinking.

"Of course it is," Charis contradicted. "Oh, Ajanta, it is so very, very exciting that you have found love with such a romantic man. And every day as you grow more and more fond of each other, you will know it is I who brought such delight into your lives."

Ajanta had a suspicion that Charis was quoting from some novel she had recently read, but as she could hardly deny what she was saying she merely shut her eyes and pretended to go to sleep.

She did in fact doze for a little while and was awoken by a sudden shriek from Charis as she exclaimed:

"Look! Look! Have you ever seen anything so marvellous?"

Ajanta woke up with a start and do did the Vicar.

They looked in the direction at which Charis was pointing.

Not far away they could see through the trees an enormous and very impressive building.

It had a centre block with high Corinthian pillars standing above a long flight of steps while on each side there were two other blocks, both surmounted by stone urns and statues which were silhouetted against the sky.

The Marquis's standard was floating from the highest point on the roof and behind the house was a wood of dark fir trees which seemed to protect it as if it was a jewel in a velvet setting.

"I have never seen anything so lovely!" Charis said. "That is where you will live, Ajanta, and reign like a Queen."

"And be dethroned like one!" Ajanta wanted to reply.

It was impossible all the same to deny that Charis's enthusiasm was well justified.

81

Stowe Hall was very beautiful and as they drew nearer they saw that the green lawns sloped down to a large lake on which there floated both white and black swans.

The bridge which spanned the lake was very much older than the house itself and beautiful beyond compare.

Because it was all so awe-inspiring, everybody in the carriage was silent as it drew up outside the front door.

Servants in green and yellow livery, which Ajanta thought must also be the Marquis's racing colours, came hurrying down the steps to attend them.

As she walked up to the front door Ajanta thought that the house, like the Marquis was overpowering and guaranteed to make anybody like herself feel small and insignificant.

But she decided she would not be intimidated by him, and when the Marquis greeted them in the Hall she was holding her chin up and he thought, as he had expected, there was a challenge in her vivid blue eyes.

"Welcome to Stowe," he said, "and I do hope your journey has not been too tiring."

"I guessed you would have an enormous and wonderful house like this!" Charis enthused before anybody else could speak. "We have had a glorious journey, a delicious luncheon, and you were so very, very clever to think of everything we might want."

"I am glad about that," the Marquis said.

He shook hands with the Vicar saying:

"It is delightful to have you here, Sir, and I know the first thing you will want to see is my Library. My curator has already a large selection of books on the Mohammedans waiting for your perusal."

He then held out his hand to Ajanta.

"There is no need for me to tell you how much I have been looking forward to seeing you," he said.

She realised from the way he raised his voice a little that he intended his welcome to be overheard by his servants.

She curtsied but made no reply, and hoped anyone

82

watching would merely think she was shy.

"Now what would you like to do first?" the Marquis asked. "Go upstairs and take off your bonnets? Or come into the Salon where I have a glass of champagne waiting for those who are old enough and some lemonade for those who are not?"

"I am thirsty!" Darice said before anybody else could speak.

"Then lemonade and some delicious chocolate cakes are waiting for you," the Marquis said.

Darice gave a little skip of joy and put her hand into the Marquis's

"You are very kind," she said. "I wish I was old enough to marry you."

"You will find in a few years there are plenty of men much more exciting than I am," the Marquis replied.

"Charis thinks you are the most exciting man in the world," Darice replied, "and so do I!"

The Marquis could not help looking at Ajanta who had a mocking smile on her lips.

He was well aware why she had not spoken since her arrival, and was sure that while she found it impossible to find fault she had wanted to do so in order to prove her independence.

Because he was so experienced where women were concerned he knew by the way she walked and the angle at which she held her head that she was fighting against being overawed by him and his house, his arrangements and the fact that her family had succumbed to his charm.

"I will make her do the same," the Marquis told himself. "Why should she be the odd one out?"

The Salon was a beautifully proportioned room and contained some extremely fine pictures.

It was impossible for Ajanta not to feel them drawing her irresistibly, so that it was difficult for her to listen to what was being said and prevent her eyes from straying from one picture to another.

"I am looking forward," the Marquis said, "to showing you round my house and describing the treasures that have been accumulated over several generations by my fore-bears, who all had acquisitive habits."

"That was fortunate for you," the Vicar commented. "I am afraid as a nation we have purloined from a great many countries their treasures to our advantage."

"And it is a magnificent heritage for our children," the Marquis said.

"Well, your son will be a very lucky young man," the Vicar replied. "He will not only have treasures that are acclaimed all over the world, but what is very important, you will teach him to appreciate them."

"Yes, of course," the Marquis agreed.

He felt this conversation so soon about any son he might have must be embarrassing for Ajanta, and he was not surprised when putting down the glass of champagne from which she had taken only a small sip, she said:

"I think, if it is convenient, I would like to go upstairs and take off my bonnet and travelling-cloak. I feel I am very untidy in comparison with such magnificence."

She did not make the last words sound exactly like a compliment, and the Marquis with his eyes twinkling, said:

"You must forgive me if I have not had a chance to tell you that you outshine everything I possess and make even my most treasured pictures pale beside the glory of your hair!"

He saw as he spoke the flash in her eyes which told him without words what she thought of his play-acting.

Charis however, gave a cry of delight and clapped her hands.

"That is really poetical!" she said. "You ought to write it down so that Ajanta will never be able to forget such beautiful words."

"I am sure she will not do that," the Marquis said.

Without replying Ajanta walked towards the door.

He opened it for her and as he walked beside her into the Hall he said:

"I was only teasing you, which I am afraid I find irresistible."

"I am glad I amuse you, My Lord!" Ajanta said coldly.

"Later I want to talk to you alone," the Marquis replied in a low voice, "but now I will send somebody to show you to your room."

He summoned as he spoke a footman who was on duty at the far end of the Hall and hurried to obey the raising of his finger.

"Take Miss Tiverton upstairs to Mrs. Flood," he said.

"Very good, M'Lord."

The footman went ahead, and as Ajanta started to follow him without looking at the Marquis there was a cry from the Salon door and Charis and Darice who had been finishing their chocolate cakes, came running across the Hall.

"Wait for us," Charis cried.

They ran up the stairs and when they found Ajanta they each took one of her hands to walk on either side of her.

'At least we are here together,' Ajanta thought and it was comforting.

CHAPTER FOUR

Upstairs the Housekeeper, Mrs. Flood, showed Ajanta into a very beautiful room which was so exquisitely furnished that apart from the bed it was hard to believe that it was not a Sitting-Room.

The sofa and chairs had gilt frames and there was a French commode of the Louis XV period which Ajanta had always longed to see.

Her mother had taught her not only about Art but also about period furniture, and she was thrilled that she could recognise many pieces which until this moment she had known only from her mother's description or from illustrations.

"I expect you would like to change, Miss," Mrs. Flood said as Ajanta took off her bonnet and travelling-cape.

"Has my luggage arrived?" she enquired.

"Yes, Miss, but there's no reason for you to wear one of the gowns that'll have been creased by packing. Your gowns from London are in the wardrobe."

As she spoke Mrs. Flood opened the doors of a very finely carved cupboard and Ajanta saw that a number of gowns were hanging inside it.

Mrs. Flood took them out one by one and she knew as she looked at them they were not only more fashionable than anything she had ever seen but so stylishly made and so prettily ornamented that she could hardly believe they were for her.

However, when she had put one on she knew that she

looked quite different and certainly more attractive than ever before in her whole life.

She had no idea until now that she had such a tiny waist, or that a gown without being in the least immodest would accentuate the perfection of her figure.

"You look lovely, Miss, and that's the truth!" Mrs. Flood said admiringly.

"Thank you," Ajanta replied.

"His Lordship's ordered tea in the Blue Drawing-Room and a footman is waiting to show you there."

"Thank you," Ajanta said again.

As she went down the stairs she felt shy and she also wondered what her father would say when he heard that the Marquis had given her some new gowns.

She found however that her family and the Marquis were not in the Blue Drawing-Room but in the Library.

The Vicar was already turning over the books which the Curator had selected for him and making exclamations of delight at finding rare volumes which, as he kept saying, would be of inestimable value in his research.

As Ajanta came in through the door to join them she saw the expression on the Marquis's face and knew he approved of her appearance.

Although she told herself she must be very grateful for his kindness, she could not help resenting the fact that he was making a puppet out of her and she was dancing to his command.

It was however Charis who recognised that she looked so different.

"Ajanta! Where did you get that gown?" she asked in a whisper.

"His Lordship gave it to me," Ajanta answered, "but do not say anything in front of Papa."

She realised that her father was unlikely to notice her appearance when he had books to look at.

When the Marquis took them into the Blue Drawing-Room for tea, he stayed behind to talk to the Curator, and

Ajanta felt a difficult moment had been avoided.

In the Blue Drawing-Room the table was set with a magnificent display of silver tea-things beside every sort of cake and sandwich that it was possible to imagine.

"Will you pour out?" the Marquis asked. "It is something you will have to get used to."

As Ajanta sat down in front of the silver tray and put out her hand towards the tea-pot, Charis exclaimed:

"It is so exciting to think, Ajanta, that you will be the mistress of this house and hostess at lots of parties! Please, will you let me come to some of them too?"

"Of course you can," the Marquis replied, before Ajanta could speak.

"And me?" Darice asked.

"We must certainly have a party in which you are included," the Marquis replied.

Darice gave a little cry of delight.

"I want to have balloons and crackers at my party," she said. "That is what one of our friends at home had, but she did not ask me, because I was too young."

"You will not be too young for the party I give," the Marquis said.

Ajanta frowned.

She thought all this talk of parties would be certain to end in disappointment.

He had said their pretended engagement might be for six months or perhaps only three.

While the sort of parties which Charis and Darice were envisaging were those which usually took place in the winter.

She was quite certain that by then they would be home in the Vicarage with nobody to entertain them and the girls would be bitterly disappointed.

It struck her that while the Marquis thought he was being generous and of course condescending to the children of an impoverished Vicar, he was really giving them a taste of something which would soon be taken from them and which they would perhaps yearn after for the rest of their lives.

"Money can be a menace if it affects one's personality and character," Ajanta told herself.

She was suddenly desperately afraid of what would be the outcome of this deception in which she was involved.

She finished pouring out the tea and when Charis passed her the dish of cucumber sandwiches she shook her head.

"Oh, do eat something, Ajanta," Charis begged. "This food is like ambrosia and we have never tasted anything like it before."

"You all three look as if you have climbed up onto Mount Olympus," the Marquis said.

"Gods and goddesses usually came *down* from Olympus to be amongst ordinary mortals!" Ajanta corrected.

The Marquis smiled.

"I am well aware that you are rebuking me, Ajanta," he said. "At the same time I thought you might have conceded that figuratively speaking Stowe Hall is Olympus."

"Only of course, as far as we are concerned."

"Exactly!" he replied mockingly.

Once again they were challenging each other and duelling with words, which he found pleasantly stimulating.

After tea he took them on a tour of some of the State Rooms of the house and he found it surprising that Ajanta knew so much about the pictures, the furniture and even the tapestries.

When she told Darice the story illustrated by one of the tapestries which even he did not know, he asked:

"How is it possible that you are so well-informed? If you were a man I should think that you had been to a University."

"Mere women can think and also read," Ajanta flashed.

"Most of them do neither," the Marquis answered.

He thought as he spoke that this was true of the women he had known.

Leone, attractive though she was, never read anything

89

except the social columns in the newspapers, and he felt the same could be said about the other women he had found alluring and desirable for a short time.

"I am becoming more and more afraid, Ajanta," he said aloud, "that you will turn out to be that terrifying creature known as a 'blue-stocking', in which case I promise you I shall run for the hills!"

Charis gave a little cry.

"Are you saying that you are not going to marry Ajanta after all? Oh, please, if you do not it will make us all very, very unhappy."

Ajanta's eyes met the Marquis's and he knew only too well what she was thinking.

"I was only teasing your sister," he said soothingly to Charis, "and clever though she is, let me assure you that I am cleverer still. So I shall not run away but try to defeat her in every argument we have together."

Charis slipped her hand into his.

"I will not argue with you," she said. "I like to listen to you, and I think everything you say is wonderful!"

The Marquis thought this was the kind of attention he usually received from older women and again he looked provocatively at Ajanta.

But she had turned away, with the little flounce of her skirts which had amused him before, to stare at a picture they had not yet inspected.

When they went upstairs to dress for dinner Darice was tired, and to Ajanta's relief there was a tray of delicious food waiting in her bedroom.

"It makes me feel hungry," Charis said.

"It is for me!" Darice replied. "All for me!"

"Of course it is," Ajanta agreed, "and Charis, you will spoil your dinner if you eat anything now."

"It is so exciting to be dining in a house like this!" Charis said. "Oh, Ajanta, I am so thrilled that you are marrying the Marquis! And if we are to live here with you it will be the most marvellous, glorious thing that could ever happen to us."

There was a little pause before Ajanta said:

"What about. .Papa?"

She saw the expression in Charis's eyes and felt as if she had struck her sister.

"You are not saying," she asked in a low voice, "that while you live here Darice and I are to go back to the Vicarage? Oh, Ajanta, how could you be so cruel and unkind to us?"

Ajanta did not speak and she went on:

"You know Papa, when he is writing he would not even remember we were there and we would be so lonely and miserable without you."

With difficulty Ajanta managed to say:

"I am not married yet. There is plenty of time to consider such things later on. Go and change, Charis, while I put Darice to bed."

"I will come to your room when I am ready," Charis said, "and if you have another new gown, I shall be very jealous!"

When Darice had eaten her supper she was in fact, very sleepy because it had been a long day for her.

She knelt on her bed and said her prayers for Ajanta as she had done ever since she was a baby, and when she cuddled down against the pillows she said:

"Goodnight, Ajanta! I love you, I love the Marquis, and this is a very happy house."

She shut her eyes and by the time Ajanta had drawn the curtains she was asleep.

Ajanta thought it was considerate of the Marquis to have put Darice in the room next to hers which was actually the dressing-room, and Charis was only one door away in another large and beautiful room.

To see that she was all right Ajanta opened her door to peep in before she began to change.

As she did so Charis gave a scream and Ajanta saw to

her surprise that Mrs. Flood and a housemaid were with her.

"Ajanta! Ajanta!" Charis cried. "Come and see what the Marquis has bought for me!"

Ajanta went into the room and saw Mrs. Flood was holding up a gown, as she had held up the ones that had arrived for her, which she had obviously just taken out of the wardrobe.

It was exactly the sort of evening-gown that a girl of sixteen should wear, but it was obviously expensively simple and could only have been designed by a dressmaker patronised by the *Beau Monde*.

"Look at it! Look at it!" Charis was saying. "Can you imagine anything more wonderful, Ajanta?"

"I'm sure it will fit the young lady," Mrs. Flood said, "but if it needs a few alterations, Elsie here is very nimble with her fingers."

"It is very pretty," Ajanta managed to say.

When she went to her own room she was however feeling angry with the Marquis because she felt he was in a way bribing her family as he had bribed her.

He may have thought he was producing a Play at Drury Lane or the Opera House, but what he was really doing was compelling her whole family by bribery and corruption into dancing to the tune he played.

"When the Marquis no longer needs us," Ajanta thought, 'he will throw us away as easily as he has picked us up, without even considering how many hearts he will break in the process."

It struck her that was what he did to the women who undoubtedly had played a large part in his life.

But if they were heart-broken, they were old enough to look after themselves, while Charis and Darice were too young and unsophisticated, and would be disillusioned and doubtless for a time, extremely unhappy.

Ignoring the maid who was waiting to help her change, Ajanta walked to the window to stand looking out at the park and the lake with its black and white swans moving serenely over the still water.

The sun was sinking in a blaze of glory and not only was the sky crimson and gold with its radiance, but it seemed as if everything else was vivid as if touched by fire.

It was very beautiful, and yet it seemed to Ajanta as if it warned her of danger, the danger of what she was doing, the danger of subterfuge, the danger of stepping out of her own particular little world into the one occupied by the Marquis.

"I have been very foolish to agree to this," she said. "I did try not to at the beginning."

She thought it had in fact been a battle between them in which she had been defeated.

Because she was worried about her sister and about her own immediate future, she found it difficult to enthuse as she should have done over the beautiful gown that the maid brought from the wardrobe for her to put on.

Mrs. Flood and Charis came into the room just as Ajanta was being buttoned up at the back, and it was their admiration as well as her reflection in the mirror which told her how becoming the gown was.

The material of which it was made, was exactly the blue of her eyes, and she wondered if the Marquis could have described her appearance in the order he sent to London or whether it was just coincidence.

Then she told herself he had done it doubtless to display his organising ability and it was annoying that anybody should be so efficient in every detail of what he had arranged.

"If there's one thing of which I'm sure," Mrs. Flood said, "it's that His Lordship's never had two lovelier young ladies to dine with him."

"Is that true?" Charis asked.

"Cross my heart it's the truth!" Mrs. Flood said, "but it's His Lordship who should be paying you compliments, not me."

She looked meaningfully at Ajanta as she spoke who was aware that Mrs. Flood and she suspected all the servants in the house were wondering why they had been invited and if there was any ulterior motive for it.

If what the Marquis had said was right, the announcement of their engagement would have been in the 'Gazette' yesterday, and copied by the other newspapers today.

They would not arrive in the country until late in the evening, or as at home, a day late.

'The household will know tomorrow, at any rate,' she thought and felt it would be very embarrassing.

When she and Charis reached the Silver Salon where they were all to assemble before dinner, they found the Marquis and their father were already there.

Ajanta had not seen the Marquis in evening-clothes before, and if he had looked handsome and magnificent in his day-clothes, at the moment he looked so distinguished that it was hard not to stare at him.

He was wearing the long black pantaloons introduced by the Prince Regent, and a frilled cravat with the points of his collar above his chin made him look even taller than he was already.

She was feeling shy about her own appearance, but Charis rushed down the room towards the Marquis to say:

"Thank you, thank you! When I saw this gown I thought I was dreaming. I do not know how to tell you how thrilled I am!"

"You look very pretty!" the Marquis said with a good humoured smile.

"Just look at me!" Charis said.

She flung out her arms to show off her gown, then pirouetted in front of him.

Her father looked at her in mild astonishment.

"Is that a new gown, Charis?" he asked.

"Of course it is, Papa! A present from the Marquis! He is the kindest man in the whole world!"

"I think that is true," the Vicar replied. "He has already given me books which I value more than a new gown, and which will have pride of place in my Library when I return home."

Ajanta's lips tightened.

She thought it only remained to see what the Marquis had in store for Lyle and Darice.

She did not have to wait long for that information.

Her father put out his hand towards her and said:

"Ajanta, my dearest, your *fiancé* has been very generous, very generous indeed!"

"What has he given you, Papa, besides books?" Ajanta asked in a tight little voice.

"He has promised me a carriage and a horse to replace my gig and poor old Bessie and, what I know will please you, another two horses for Lyle and Charis to ride and a pony for Darice."

"A horse for me?" Charis said. "Then I shall be able to go hunting! Oh, it is marvellous! Marvellous!"

She flung her arms around the Marquis as she spoke and kissed his cheek.

He kissed hers in return, then he said:

"If you are so effusive for the present of a horse, I am wondering what you will say when you receive a diamond necklace!"

"I would much rather have a horse so that I can go out and meet people," Charis replied.

The Marquis laughed.

"I have a feeling that you are already looking for adventure and doubtless for strangers like myself to save you this time from unfortunate accidents in the hunting-field."

"Oh, I do hope so!" Charis cried, and the Marquis laughed again.

He was however well aware of Ajanta's disapproval and as he brought her a glass of champagne he said:

"You are very silent, Ajanta!"

"Do you really need my paeans of praise to be added to Papa's and Charis's?" she enquired.

"Of course!" he replied. "As you well know, what you say and think is very important to me, and as the newspapers arrived twenty minutes ago everybody in the house will now be aware why I am seeking your approval in everything I do."

"You may have to coach me in my lines."

"Of course I am willing to do that," he replied, "but I warn you that as the producer I expect perfection."

"It will be very sad if I fail to live up to the standards you have set yourself," Ajanta answered.

She thought the Marquis intended to say something sharp as if he felt she was trying his patience too far, when her father joined them.

"I was just wondering," he said, "when we shall have the pleasure of meeting your family? I presume you have told them of your intentions with regard to my daughter?"

"I sent a note to my mother who lives in the Dower House," the Marquis replied, "and the rest of my relations will know tonight."

"I am glad about that," the Vicar said. "I have always found that families are upset and often feel insulted if they are not told about an engagement before it becomes public knowledge."

The Marquis glanced at Ajanta and they were both thinking the same thing.

They were saved however from making any reply because at that moment the Butler announced dinner.

Ajanta was not surprised that as course succeeded course in the beautiful Dining-Room each dish was more delectable than the last.

Even Charis was silent as she ate, and Ajanta thought that perhaps the Marquis was right in saying he had taken them to Olympus, although it annoyed her that he should be so pleased with himself and his possessions.

And yet she was honest enough to admit that he had every reason to be.

As he was undeniably so handsome, charming, she could understand why Charis looked at him with admiring eyes and she had never seen her father look so relaxed and happy since her mother had died.

"I am afraid," the Marquis said as they finished dinner, "that this is the last meal we shall have alone for the next few days."

"Why is that?" the Vicar asked.

"Because some of my relations will be arriving for luncheon and dinner tomorrow, and doubtless batches of others will invite themselves in the following days until Ajanta and I will be sick to death of receiving their good wishes."

"I am sure they will be very sincere," the Vicar said. "Relations, I find, always want the bachelor in the family to be married."

The Marquis laughed.

"That is true. If they are caught in the bonds of matrimony themselves, they cannot bear anybody else to be free and unconfined."

The Vicar smiled.

"I think," he said, "whatever your relations may think, you have been wise, my dear Quintus, to wait until the right woman came along. I was fortunate to find my wife when we were both young."

He sighed before he added:

"It gave us longer together and a joy and happiness that was inexpressible. Other men however, have to wait, as you have done, but you know now it was worth waiting for."

"Yes, indeed," the Marquis agreed.

"Ajanta is so very, very lucky!" Charis said. "I want to marry somebody just like you. I wish you had a brother."

"That is something I have often wished for myself," the Marquis said. "It is very lonely being an only child, and I envy you, Charis, having two sisters and a brother."

"When shall we see Lyle?" Charis asked.

"Tomorrow," the Marquis replied. "I sent a groom over to Oxford this afternoon to ask him to join us and if it was possible to stay until Sunday night."

"That was kind of you," Ajanta said and there was a light in her eyes that had not been there before.

"I am glad I have pleased you," the Marquis replied, and knowing that mentally he was adding: 'At last!' she felt a little ashamed of herself.

"I am well aware," she said, "of all the thought you have given us, and I am not really ungrateful."

Her eyes met his as she spoke and she had a feeling that he was perceptively aware that her words had not been completely sincere, and she was in fact, because of the secret that lay between them, not really grateful, but resentful.

After dinner was finished and they were all sitting in the Silver Salon the Vicar left them to collect a book from the Library that he particularly wished to read when he went to bed.

Because she was so excited Charis found it difficult to sit still, so she went with him leaving the Marquis and Ajanta alone.

He looked at her sitting rather stiffly in the brocade chair which framed the beauty of her gown, while the lights from the crystal chandelier glittered on the gold of her hair and made it shine almost dazzlingly.

It struck him that when she was fashionably gowned she would undoubtedly hold her own with all the beautiful women he entertained in his house, even Leone.

Then he told himself that while he admired Ajanta's beauty she was vastly different in character and personality from any woman to whom he had made love.

"Far too prickly, far too provocative for me," the Marquis told himself.

Then because he found he could not resist duelling with her in words, he said:

"As my leading lady, may I point out, Ajanta, that I am disappointed with your acting ability."

"Disappointed?" Ajanta questioned. "What have I done wrong?"

"Your role is very simple," he said. "You are a young unsophisticated woman living in the country, who has attracted the attention of the sophisticated, bored and blasé Marquis of Stowe."

Ajanta's lips quivered and she gave a little laugh, but she did not interrupt and the Marquis went on:

"In a whirlwind courtship he sweeps her off her feet and she promises to marry him. To express his love, he brings her silks and satins to clothe her, and shows her his inexhaustible treasures which she is to share with him in their future life."

The Marquis paused and because she could not help being amused by what he was saying Ajanta prompted:

"Do go on. I want to hear the next Act."

"I am concerned with my leading lady's feelings," the Marquis said reflectively.

"I apologise for interrupting you. The script, may I say, was not very clear."

"Then my directions should leave no possible question of doubt," the Marquis said. "The country girl is overwhelmed, captivated, and very much in love. She thinks the noble Marquis is a Knight in Shining Armour, come to rescue her from the boredom and monotony of her narrow existence."

"So she gapes at him like a gabble-cock!" Ajanta interposed.

"A gabble-cock?" the Marquis enquired.

"The local name for a turkey," Ajanta explained, and saw his eyes twinkle.

"Gaping like a gabble-cock," he went on, "she is aware when she is carried away by her Knight to his Palace that her heart beats tumultuously! She finds herself admiring everything he does, everything he says, because,

after all, it would be impossible for her to criticis
perfection!"

Ajanta's laughter rang out.

"What a glorious fairy-tale!" she exclaimed. "Now o
course I understand where I am going wrong, but the troubl
is I doubt my own capabilities, and perhaps, in fact I am sur
you have cast the wrong person for the part."

The Marquis lying back in his chair with his legs crosse
looked Ajanta up and down, as if searching for faults.

"You certainly look right," he said. "No leading lad
transformed by her Fairy Godmother could look mor
alluring. At the same time, you have forgotten to disguis
your eyes."

"My eyes?" Ajanta echoed.

"I can see emotions expressed in them which my heroin
would certainly not feel," the Marquis answered, "conden
nation, dissatisfaction, and undoubtedly sometimes dislike!

"That is not true!" Ajanta said hotly. "I do not dislike yo
I just feel. . ."

She paused for words.

"Feel what?" the Marquis prompted.

"That you are playing a dangerous game, not from you
own point of view, but from ours."

"What do you mean by that?"

"I know as you honestly pointed out," Ajanta answered
"that this is a Play which will run for a month, perhaps tw
or three, then will abruptly be taken off, and the supportin
cast will be turned out of the Theatre without a chance o
being re-employed."

Her voice altered as she went on:

"They will also be aware that never. .never again wi
they enjoy the. .glamour and the. .glory of taking part i
such a. .resplendent Show! It will be. .very hurtful."

There was a little tremor in Ajanta's voice as she said th
last words.

Then as she looked at the Marquis she realised that thi
was something he had not considered and he wa

contemplating the point she had made for the first time.

In a different tone from the one he had used before he said:

"I understand what you are saying to me, Ajanta, and let me promise you one thing; I will try not to hurt anybody unnecessarily but, as you are well aware, sometimes in life it is unavoidable."

"It is something from which we should all try to. .protect. .those we. .love," Ajanta said quickly.

The Marquis did not reply, but she knew she had given him something to think about as her father came back into the Salon carrying the book he had collected from the Library.

. . . .

The following day everything seemed to happen so quickly that there was no time for introspection and there was not a moment when she could have a private conversation with the Marquis.

In the morning horses were provided for them to ride after breakfast and although Ajanta had to wear her old threadbare habit which she had almost grown out of, she had given no thought to her appearance. She was riding one of the finest horses she had ever seen, with Charis in a wild state of excitement riding beside her.

Before they left Darice was taken to the paddock to try out two ponies and find which suited her best.

When she learned that the one she chose was a gift that she could keep for ever she cried because she was so happy.

"I have – always wanted – one – you know I have – Ajanta!" she sobbed.

"There is nothing to cry about," Ajanta said.

"Because I have – wanted one – so much – I cannot – believe that now it is – really – mine!" Darice said.

She held out her arms to the Marquis as she spoke and he picked her up.

"If the pony is going to make you cry I shall take it away again," he said.

"I – always want to – cry when I am very – very happy," Darice explained.

"Then you must laugh when things go wrong and you are not happy," the Marquis said.

She smiled at him through her tears.

"That would be a – topsy-turvy way of – doing things."

"So is crying when you ought to be jumping for joy."

"I will jump on my pony," Darice said as he lifted her onto the saddle.

They watched as the groom, taking her on a leading rein, moved away with her, then they mounted their own horses and set off to ride through the Park.

"I was certain you would both be outstanding riders," the Marquis remarked.

"If we are it is surprising," Charis replied. "Sharing Rover with Ajanta is frustrating enough, but in the holidays Lyle wants him every day and we have to walk."

"That is something you will not have to do in the future," the Marquis said.

"That is what I thought in the night," Charis answered, "and I pinched myself in case I was dreaming."

When a little later they turned back towards the Hall the Marquis said to Ajanta:

"I think you will find somebody you very much want to see waiting for you when we reach home."

He saw a light he had never seen before in her eyes, and the expression on her face, he told himself, was what his relatives would expect to see when she looked at him.

"For luncheon," he warned her, "there will be two uncles, three cousins and a terrifying old aunt of mine. So do not forget that they will be extremely curious and undoubtedly ready to be critical."

"You are frightening me!"

"Only warning you," the Marquis replied, "and if you find my relatives a bore, remember, I have suffered from them for thirty-three years!"

"Are you as old as that?" Ajanta asked. "I am not surprised they have almost given up saving money for a wedding present."

"We had better make it quite clear that we do not expect wedding presents to arrive so quickly," the Marquis said, 'otherwise we shall have to write letters of thanks to them."

"*You* will have to write them," Ajanta corrected. "They will be presents for you, not me."

"I think they are usually accepted jointly," the Marquis replied, "and unless it is a very close relative they will expect to hear from you. After all, it is the woman's job to make herself pleasant."

He thought that Ajanta would not let such a remark pass and he was not disappointed.

"I think that is typical of a man's inclination to make a woman do all the dull things in a marriage, while he does all the amusing and gayest ones."

"What do you mean by that?" the Marquis enquired.

"From what I have read of those who live in society," Ajanta replied, "I gather it is the woman who stays at home, entertains the correct people, patronises orphans and the elderly, besides supporting any other charities with which she and her husband are concerned."

The Marquis was listening with an amused smile as she went on;

"For a man it is quite different. He has race-meetings, prize-fights and his Clubs to attend. He can be away from home for long stretches at a time without expecting any complaints."

She gave the Marquis a knowing little glance before she went on:

"What is more, according to what I have heard, he often goes abroad when the country is not at war, not taking his wife because she might find the journey uncomfortable and largely because he simply wishes to get away!"

"And where have you learnt all this?" the Marquis asked.

"Are you saying it is not true?"

"I am only amused that among the cabbages you should have developed such an astute appraisement of social life as lived by the nobility."

"Even the cabbages have ears," Ajanta replied, "and birds carry gossip from one nest to another."

"From what you have said that must undoubtedly be true," the Marquis answered, "and again you are stepping out of character, Ajanta. My country heroine is wide-eyed and adoring, and sees no wrong in her hero, nor would he ever disappoint her by going abroad alone."

"I am not saying he goes alone," Ajanta said provocatively. "I only said he is not accompanied by his wife."

She knew as she spoke that she had surprised the Marquis. Then the expression on his face changed, and his eyes twinkled.

"You have certainly convinced me that my script will have to be re-written," he said ruefully.

It was what Ajanta had hoped to make him feel and she touched her horse lightly with her whip to make him move quicker so that she would not have to say any more.

It was one of her teachers who had first told her about the social world, having been, before she retired, a Governess in several noble families.

She made Ajanta work hard at the subjects her mother wished her to study.

But there was nothing the old woman enjoyed more than a gossip and when the lesson was over she would chat away for as long as Ajanta could stay about the old days, and the things that took place in the big houses in which she had taught.

Ajanta had learnt a great deal not only about the behaviour of the older members of society who had been Miss Caruthers' employers but also about the young married couples who came to stay in the house and the raffish parties which took place when the oldest son entertained his friends.

She had found it all fascinating and a world which she thought she would never know, and which to her was like listening to one of Sir Walter Scott's novels being read aloud and in it an intersection of Jane Austen's heroes and heroines.

Because Ajanta was in a hurry to reach the Hall she rode so quickly that it was hard for the Marquis and Charis to keep up with her.

Then as she reached the flight of stone steps she saw somebody standing at the top of them and she knew it was Lyle.

Pulling her horse to a standstill she called out his name excitedly.

"Lyle! Lyle!"

"Hello, Ajanta!"

He ran down the steps to lift her down and she kissed his cheek affectionately. But his eyes were on the horse she had been riding.

"What a beauty!" he exclaimed. "I cannot wait to see the Marquis's stable!"

"I have not seen it yet," Ajanta answered, "but I am sure there will be plenty of horses for you to admire and to ride."

Lyle turned his handsome face from contemplation of the horse he was caressing to ask:

"Is it really true you are to marry him?"

Just for a moment Ajanta contemplated telling her brother the truth.

Then reluctantly, because she knew she must not break her word, she said:

"Yes. .we are engaged."

CHAPTER FIVE

When Ajanta woke the following morning she lay thinking of the happiness of the previous evening.

Despite the fact that she was well aware the Marquis's relations were looking her over as if she was a horse, and taking note of her good points, she felt gay and relaxed.

That was because Lyle was there and he was in high spirits.

He had been able to ride one of the Marquis's superb horses in the afternoon and had taken him over the abbreviated steeple-chase course which the Marquis had erected in the Park.

"I was right in guessing you were all superlative riders," the Marquis said to Ajanta as Lyle took a very high fence in a manner which made her want to applaud.

"None of us are as good as Lyle."

"I can see he is a hero in your eyes," the Marquis replied, she thought a little sarcastically.

"I love him!" Ajanta said simply, "and he is such an exceptional person that I feel I have to look after him in the same way as I look after my father."

The Marquis looked at her for a long moment before he asked:

"Do you never think of yourself? After all, I have learnt that you are twenty, and it is time you were thinking of getting married."

"To whom?" Ajanta asked lightly. "One of the cabbages you are so rude about?"

"It might be better than remaining an old maid."

Ajanta did not reply for a moment because she was watching Lyle. Then she said:

"I suppose I have been. .hoping that like Mama I would fall in love at first sight. .but I know that is. .something in which you do not. .believe."

"Perhaps it would be truer to say it has never happened to me," the Marquis replied.

As he spoke he knew that was only true of what the words "falling in love" meant to Ajanta.

Of course it had often happened when he walked into a room and saw a beautiful woman, that he was aware he desired her and knew it was only a question of time before she became his.

Because invariably such beauties were like Leone already married, it was not the same kind of love he was discussing with Ajanta.

"But would it be so very different?" he asked himself.

He remembered that inevitably after a few months the flames of passion would die down and he found himself bored by the woman he had at first thought so desirable.

Because he was silent Ajanta turned to look at him.

"You will have to get married sometime," she said, "if only to please your relatives who I saw at luncheon were enthralled and excited that at last you had taken the plunge."

"I cannot think why they do not leave me alone," the Marquis said crossly.

"You are head of the family," Ajanta said, "and I gather from your aunt that your heir-presumptive is an exceedingly unpleasant character who has only managed to produce five very plain daughters."

"A fate that might happen to me!" the Marquis replied lightly.

"I doubt that," Ajanta said.

She spoke softly as she was looking at Lyle.

The Marquis heard her.

"Why should you doubt that possibility?"

"Not that you should have daughters. But if when you marry you are in love your sons will all be handsome and your daughters very beautiful."

The Marquis was interested.

"Explain to me exactly what you are suggesting."

Ajanta was smiling as once again she turned her head to look at him.

"Mama always believed that we were beautiful – that sounds rather conceited, but it is something you said yourself – because she and Papa were so much in love with each other."

She paused as if he would argue with her, then continued:

"She told me this when I was quite young, and I have watched other families and I certainly have found it true that where two people are very happily married and in love, their children are beautiful and healthy."

The Marquis did not say so aloud, but it flashed through his mind that 'love-children' were always, if history was to be believed, as Ajanta had described.

Then he thought of Lady Sarah and was sure that the Duke's marriage to the Duchess had been arranged because their two families thought it an appropriate match.

"What you have said certainly makes me worry about my future," he said, speaking a little mockingly.

"I would like you to be happy," Ajanta replied, "because you are so kind and generous. I think that when you do decide to be married you should hope that fate or the gods, whichever you believe in, will send you somebody who will capture your heart and you will live happily ever afterwards."

Because she was speaking seriously the Marquis did not laugh. Instead he said:

"Thank you, Ajanta. I shall remember what you said."

There was no time for them to talk any more.

Lyle flushed and excited came riding back to them and

the Marquis and Ajanta mounted their own horses and galloped away over the Park.

More relatives came to dinner and again everything was far easier than Ajanta had anticipated.

There was one elderly cousin who had been a great traveller, and he and the Vicar had so much to say to each other that it was difficult to gouge them apart.

The ladies, far from being condescending, as Ajanta had expected, were charming to her.

A young cousin who had come unexpectedly with his father and mother monopolised Charis, who by the end of the evening, was starry-eyed and undoubtedly, Ajanta thought, falling in love again.

"You are very clever, dearest," Lyle said to Ajanta as he kissed her goodnight. "I cannot imagine how living in the wilds of nowhere you could find anybody so attractive, so generous and such a fine sportsman as the Marquis."

"You must thank Charis for that," Ajanta replied.

"Charis!" Lyle exclaimed. "We will have to do something about that young woman, Ajanta. She was making eyes at young Storrington in a way which made me feel quite embarrassed."

"She is at a romantic age."

Lyle smiled. Then he said:

"I think the truth is that because of Mama and Papa we all are. As a matter of fact, I think I am falling in love myself!"

"Oh, no, Lyle, no!" Ajanta exclaimed.

"Why not?" Lyle asked. "She is the prettiest girl I have ever seen, and the only difficulty up until now has been that I could never afford to ask her out even for tea. Now all that will be changed."

He smiled as he finished:

"You have told me that I can have some decent clothes and an allowance which will at least permit me to take a girl out occasionally. So, Ajanta, I am dancing in the sky!"

Ajanta wanted to add a word of warning that, as the Marquis had said, such affluence would not last for ever.

Once again she was worried because their way of life had changed so dramatically, but she could not tell Lyle it had a limited existence.

Anyway it was difficult to think of anything but how thrilling it was to have her whole family with her to enjoy the Marquis's good food, the Marquis's house, and of course the Marquis's horses.

'We had better make hay while the sun shines,' she thought before she fell asleep.

. . . .

When she awoke she could hear the birds singing and thought their song was echoed in her heart.

Then as she was listening to them the door opened quietly and a maid came in to draw back the curtains and place a pot of fragrant China tea beside her bed.

When Ajanta sat up to drink it she saw there was a note propped against the tea-pot.

She wondered who it was from, opened it and read what was written in astonishment.

"If you care for the person to whom you are engaged, if you value his happiness and want to save him from disgrace, you will meet me not later than seven o'clock at the edge of the wood that borders the North of the Park. This is very, very urgent!"

There was no heading to the letter and no signature. Ajanta read it again thinking it must be some sort of a joke.

She made a note of the time she had to meet this stranger and as she looked at the clock over the mantelpiece the maid, who was tidying the room, said:

"I called you early, Miss, because the person who left the note said it was imperative that you should receive it at once."

"What is the correct time?" Ajanta asked, thinking the clock must be wrong.

"Just after six o'clock, Miss. I hope I did right in bringing you the note immediately."

"Yes, of course," Ajanta said.

She read what was written again and thought there was nothing she could do but meet the person in question. If in fact, as was insinuated some danger threatened the Marquis, she would be very remiss if she refused to help him.

She got out of bed.

"Give me my riding-habit please."

It did not take her long to dress and when she was ready she wondered if she ought to tell the Marquis where she was going.

Then she decided it would be embarrassing and might also delay her from reaching the wood in time.

Instead she went down a back staircase which the maid told her would lead to the stables and when she reached them she found the groom who had taken Darice riding the day before.

He touched his forelock.

" 'Mornin', Miss!"

"Will you please saddle me a horse?" Ajanta said. "I wish to ride alone. I will not be long."

The groom looked surprised but he was too well trained to question any order he was given.

Five minutes later Ajanta set off leaving the stable not by the front of the house as she was afraid the Marquis might see her, but out by another way which led past the paddock where the young horses were kept.

Entering the Park behind a small copse of trees, she touched the horse she was riding with her whip and galloped as quickly as she could towards the wood that she knew was on the North side.

She found a ride through the trees and as she was forced to go slower she began to worry in case this was a trap of some sort.

Supposing some enemies of the Marquis wanted to kidnap her? In that case she would look very foolish to have come here without an escort.

Then she told herself such things only happened in novels, not in real life, but she had to admit that everything that concerned the Marquis did seem stranger than fiction.

The ride took her to the other side of the wood, where waiting in the field beyond she saw a horse and riding it a woman.

Somehow she had expected her correspondent to be a man, but not only was it a woman wearing an exquisitely cut and very attractive riding-habit, but she was also very beautiful.

When she saw Ajanta her eyes seemed to light up and there was a surprising expression of pleasure on her beautiful face.

As Ajanta drew up her horse beside the woman's she cried:

"You have come! I was so afraid you would either refuse to do so, or else you did not exist at all!"

Ajanta looked puzzled and the lady said:

"That is what my husband believes, and that is why I had to warn you."

"I am afraid I do not. .understand."

The lady sighed.

"The Marquis has not told you about me?"

"No, and I have no idea who you are."

There was a little silence. Then the lady said:

"I somehow thought he would have explained to you why your engagement was necessary."

"He asked me to help him," Ajanta answered, "and I understood he was in some sort of trouble."

"Very great trouble indeed!" the lady said, "but I am hoping and praying that you can save him."

She looked so beautiful as she spoke that Ajanta could only stare at her before she managed to ask:

"Would you tell me who you are?"

"Yes, of course," the lady replied. "I am Lady Burnham, and my husband is – threatening to – divorce me – citing the – Marquis!"

She obviously found it hard to say the words, and the expression of pain on her face was very revealing.

"Divorce you?" Ajanta exclaimed. "But how. .terrible!"

She was aware that divorce was considered scandalous and something so outrageous and degrading that no lady with any idea of decency could bear to be involved in one.

"We had no idea," Lady Burnham said with a little sob in her voice, "that my husband was – having us – watched – and he is determined, yes – determined to have his – revenge on the – Marquis because – he hates him!"

"How can he do anything so horrible, so cruel to. .you?" Ajanta asked.

She thought it was even more horrifying because Lady Burnham was so beautiful, while the way she spoke and the tears that misted her eyes made her seem so pathetic that she wanted to comfort her.

"The main reason," Lady Burnham answered, "why my husband has always – hated the Marquis is that the Marquis's horses are – better than his own."

"Then why did you. . .?" Ajanta began, then realised it would be an impertinent question and stopped speaking.

"I fell in love," Lady Burnham said. "How could I help it when Quintus is so handsome – so attractive and so very – very – persuasive?"

Her voice broke for a moment, but she went on bravely:

"But I did not – realise that loving him could both – damage him and – destroy me!"

Ajanta thought for a moment. Then she said:

"I think, if I am not mistaken, that the Marquis hoped that by getting engaged so quickly he could prevent your husband from carrying out his intention."

It was all still a little vague in her mind, but she was sure now that this was why the Marquis had proposed their pretend engagement and offered her so much money to agree.

"Yes, of course – and it was a very – clever idea," Lady Burnham said. "But because – forgive me if this sounds rude – you are somebody – unknown – George thinks you do not – exist."

"But, I do!" Ajanta said.

"That is why I felt I had to warn Quintus," Lady Burnham said, "or rather – make you – warn him. I dare not – see him – myself."

She looked over her shoulder as she spoke and said:

"Perhaps I am being watched at this very moment! I do not know, and it was too dangerous to write him a letter. So the only chance I had of – letting him know the – truth was to – speak to – you."

As if she felt this needed further explanation she went on:

"I pretended to my husband when your engagement was announced that I had met you and had advised Quintus to marry you because you were so charming. But because he has never heard your name he is quite – certain he is being – tricked in some way."

'Which is the truth!' Ajanta thought, but aloud she asked:

"What do you want me to do?"

"I want you to be ready for my husband to – appear sometime during this – afternoon. He is going to – challenge Quintus to produce you or admit that his – engagement is just a lie."

"I cannot understand why he should think that," Ajanta said.

"My husband has got it into his head that to prevent my being divorced the Marquis is just pretending that he is to be married to a respectable young girl."

She sighed and continued:

"He is convinced Quintus has either invented someone

who does not exist or has paid some play-actress to act the part until the danger is over."

This was so near the truth that Ajanta thought Lord Burnham must be an unusually perceptive and intelligent man.

Lady Burnham sighed again.

"My husband is very obstinate and very persistent. If he once makes up his mind to take a certain course of action it is almost – impossible to make him – change his mind."

"I hope in this instance you can prevent him from doing what he intends," Ajanta said.

"I have been trying – desperately to do so," Lady Burnham replied, "and I think if George is – convinced this afternoon that he has made a mistake – then he will admit that he has been – misinformed, and that Quintus and I have done – nothing – wrong."

"Shall I tell the Marquis that Lord Burnham is coming to see him?" Ajanta asked.

Lady Burnham appeared to think for a moment.

"I think it might be better than if you appear surprised by his visit. If Quintus is obstructive or insulting, it might make him determined to go ahead with the divorce case. He has already arranged if he is not satisfied, for a Solicitor to take his case before Parliament tomorrow."

"Tomorrow?" Ajanta ejaculated.

"You do see why I am so – worried?" Lady Burnham asked. "And I had to – convince myself that you are a – real person."

She looked at Ajanta as if seeing her for the first time and said:

"You are very lovely! It was clever of Quintus to find you."

"Thank you," Ajanta answered, "and you are the most beautiful person I have ever seen!"

"How sweet of you to say that," Lady Burnham replied. 'I have been so worried and unhappy I feel I must look an – absolute freak."

"You could never look that," Ajanta answered.

Lady Burnham smiled.

"I suppose really I should be jealous that you are so beautiful but, because I love Quintus with all my heart, can only hope that you will make him very – very happy."

Ajanta felt it would be better just to say thank you.

"I must go back now," Lady Burnham went on. "If George finds out I have been away I shall merely say that am so unhappy because he will not believe me, that I went riding by myself and hoped that my horse would throw me and I would – break my – neck."

Ajanta gave a little cry.

"You must not say such things!"

"I have to be dramatic to prove my innocence!" Lady Burnham retorted. "And George will never believe me unless he is – convinced by what he – sees this – afternoon."

"I will do my very best to make sure he does," Ajanta said, "and thank you for being so brave as to warn me."

Lady Burnham turned her horse.

"Goodbye," she said. "Remember I shall be praying that everything will be all right. I cannot be divorced! If I am, I swear I will kill myself."

She did not wait for Ajanta to reply but rode off, leaving her staring after her in a bewildered fashion.

She had wondered, of course, wondered a thousand times what was the reason why the Marquis wanted to be engaged and that it should be announced within three days.

Now she knew the truth and the predicament he was in was worse than anything she had thought of.

Miss Caruthers had once, in her revelations of what happened in noble houses touched on divorce, and Ajanta could remember what had been said.

She had spoken in shocked tones when she related how one of the Duke's daughters had, because she was so

116

desperately unhappy with her husband, run away with another man.

"Of course," Miss Chamberlain said, "it meant that none of us ever mentioned her name again and the Duke behaved as if she were no longer alive."

"How horrid of him!" Ajanta exclaimed.

"No, dear, he was right," Miss Chamberlain replied. "She brought shame on her family by doing something disgraceful!"

"Did her husband divorce her?" Ajanta asked.

"He contemplated doing so, but His Grace dissuaded him on the ground that it would cause a scandal which would affect them all."

"What happened to her?" Ajanta enquired.

Miss Chamberlain shrugged her shoulders.

"I expect she went abroad. No one in England would speak to her, and of course if she was living 'in sin' I imagine even the foreigners she would know, would be of no social consequence."

It seemed to Ajanta at the time a very cruel fate and she felt she could almost understand why Lady Burnham would rather be dead than in such a position.

At the same time, she could not help feeling that she and the Marquis must have realised the consequences of what they were doing if they were found out.

'They were breaking one of the Ten Commandments,' she thought.

Because Lady Burnham was so lovely she could understand the Marquis being attracted to her, and because he was so handsome it was not surprising that she fell in love with him.

It all seemed rather complicated, and it was much more difficult now she had met both the people in question to condemn them for their behaviour and not sympathise with them in the predicament in which they found themselves.

117

Then she told herself it was not for her to judge what they had done, but rather to earn the large amount of money she had been paid to save them.

"It would certainly be dishonest of me if I do not try in every way I can," Ajanta reasoned, and she knew that was what she must do.

After luncheon at which again there were a number of relatives who wished her and the Marquis every happiness and toasted them frequently in his excellent wine, Ajanta made her plans.

"What are we going to do this afternoon?" Charis asked.

Ajanta had anticipated this question and to her relief after they had ridden in the morning the weather had clouded over and it had begun to rain.

There was an uncomfortable moment when as they returned from riding the Marquis had asked one of the grooms who collected the horses at the front door why Ajanta had been given a different horse from the one she had ridden the day before.

"I wanted *Mercury* to be kept exclusively for Miss Tiverton," he said.

"I know, M'Lord," the groom replied, "but as he went out with the young lady first thing this morning I felt he mightn't be able to keep up with Your Lordship."

The Marquis looked surprised and as he walked up the steps beside Ajanta he said:

"You did not tell me you had been riding before breakfast."

"I forgot," Ajanta replied and hurried up the stairs before he could question her any further.

Now she said in answer to Charis's question:

"As it is too wet to go out, I was going to ask the Marquis if he will give us a personally conducted tour of the rooms we have not already seen."

"That is a good idea," Charis said. "I will go now and ask him."

The Marquis was just leaving the Dining-Room with his

relatives and impetuously she ran towards him saying:

"Ajanta says you might take us round the house this afternoon. You know we have not seen half of it yet, and Darice and I want to climb up to the very top where there must be a wonderful view."

"There is," the Marquis smiled, "but there is a lot to see downstairs first."

One of his relatives laughed.

"I can see you will have an attentive audience, Quintus. It will make you think you are back in the war when I hear you used to lecture your troops for hours on ways they could take the enemy by surprise."

"I think you are insinuating rather obliquely that I like the sound of my own voice," the Marquis said.

"The idea never crossed my mind!" his relative replied. "But I am quite certain you would not wish to disappoint anybody so pretty as your future sister-in-law."

He put his arm around Charis's shoulder as he spoke and said:

"You are quite certain, little one, that you would not like me to be your guide?"

"If the Marquis refuses I might ask you," Charis said, "but I expect he knows more about his own house than you do."

Everybody laughed as if she had said something clever and the relation said:

"It is no use, Quintus. We have all given up competing where you are concerned."

It was a long time before everybody had said goodbye, and looking at the large grandfather clock in the Hall Ajanta began to wonder when Lord Burnham would arrive.

She had dressed herself in one of her prettiest gowns that had come from London and Charis had another attractive one that made her look exceedingly pretty, and also, Ajanta thought with satisfaction, very lady-like.

Darice with her new blue sash on a white muslin gown that had been starched and pressed by the housemaids looked as usual adorable, and she felt sure that whatever else he might think it would be impossible for Lord Burnham to imagine they were actresses from a Playhouse.

They were in the Armoury, which seemed an ironically appropriate place, when Lord Burnham was announced.

The walls were covered with ancient weapons of every sort which the Marquis's relatives had collected or actually used in the years in which they had fought.

Ancient flags hung from the cornise where it met the ceiling, and there were portraits of the Storringtons in their uniforms, looking smugly triumphant, as if they had just won a major victory.

"Lord Burnham, M'Lord!" the Butler said from the doorway, and the Marquis turned round in surprise.

After what Lady Burnham had said about him, Ajanta had somehow expected he would look very much as he did.

If the Marquis had not been present he might have passed for quite a good-looking man.

He was tall but rather thick-set, and because he was angry there was a scowl on his face and he walked towards the Marquis in a manner which was obviously aggressive.

"Good afternoon, Burnham!" the Marquis said. "This is indeed a surprise! I was not expecting you."

"I have come," Lord Burnham said in a loud voice, "to see for myself if this mythical young woman to whom you have announced your engagement actually exists."

He paused before he went on with the air of a man giving an address to a large company of people:

"It appears to me to be very strange that none of your friends have heard of her, nor has she been seen in any social circles or by anybody of my acquaintance, except of course my wife, whose word I can hardly rely on in this particular!"

"I cannot imagine why you should doubt it," the

Marquis said coolly. "Let me introduce you to my fiancée."

He turned to look back at Ajanta who deliberately had not moved from where she had been standing.

When Lord Burnham was announced she had been looking at a collection of ancient swords.

Now she walked to the Marquis's side and he said:

"Let me introduce you, Ajanta, to Lord Burnham who is anxious to make your acquaintance. My fiancée, Miss Ajanta Tiverton!"

Ajanta held out her hand.

"I am so delighted to meet you," she said. "Lady Burnham has always been so kind to me and I do hope she has come with you."

Lord Burnham stared at her.

He was not only astonished at Ajanta's looks, and in the austerity of the Armoury her hair seemed to glow as if it held little lights in it, but also what she had said was totally unexpected.

As he took her hand she dropped him a small curtsy, and as if he felt he must reply to what she had asked he said:

"No, my wife is not with me."

"Oh, I am so sorry!" Ajanta replied. "Will you please give Her Ladyship my very best love and say that when we come to London I hope I shall have the privilege of being invited to your house."

As Ajanta spoke she was aware that not only Lord Burnham was looking surprised at what she was saying, but so was the Marquis.

Then the latter was quick-witted enough to take advantage of his enemy's discomfiture.

"Now that you have met Ajanta," he said, "you must meet two other members of her family."

The girls were close at hand and the Marquis pushed Charis gently forward saying:

"This is Charis, who is sixteen, and in another year will be making her curtsy to the Queen, and this is Darice, who

121

will have to wait a little longer."

Lord Burnham stared from one to the other and for a moment it seemed as if he had nothing to say.

Then as Ajanta thought afterwards, almost as if it was on cue, the door opened and Lyle came into the Armoury.

"Oh, here you are!" he said. "I have been looking for you everywhere!"

Then he stopped and looked around.

"I say!" he ejaculated. "What an amazing display of weapons! Is there a duelling-pistol! Can I try one out?"

The Marquis laughed.

"You must try to prevent yourself from becoming engaged in a duel at least until you have gained your degree!"

He then turned to Lord Burnham to say:

"Here is another member of my fiancée's family. Let me introduce Lyle Tiverton, who is at Oxford, and has come here specially to give me his congratulations."

Lyle held out his hand eagerly.

"I have not met you before, My Lord," he said, "but I have seen you on the race-course, and I backed your runner when it won at Epsom last month. I only wish I could have been there to see him run!"

"You are keen on racing?" Lord Burnham asked.

It sounded as though his voice was rather weak and very different from the manner in which he had spoken when he arrived.

"Very, very keen," Lyle replied, "and I did watch the Derby last year when your horse came in second."

"To mine!" the Marquis said with satisfaction.

Because she felt that he was being needlessly provocative, Ajanta said quickly:

"Oh, please, Quintus, do let us ask Lord Burnham to stay to tea. I know Papa would be delighted to meet him not only because he has heard so much about his horses from Lyle, but also I am sure Lord Burnham has a Library in his

122

house which contains many magnificent volumes."

This was a shot in the dark, but she was certain that as Lord Burnham was rich he would have a Library.

"Is your father here too?" Lord Burnham asked.

"Yes, he is," Ajanta replied, "and I know he would be very gratified to meet Your Lordship. We have so often talked about you."

Lord Burnham however had heard and seen enough.

"I am afraid it will have to wait for another time," he said sharply. "I cannot keep my horses waiting."

He looked at the Marquis and although Ajanta thought there was hatred in his eyes, he managed to say wryly:

"You win, Stowe! But I am almost certain it was not a straight race!"

"If you are expecting me to be insulted and call you out," the Marquis replied, "I am sure Lyle would be delighted for me to do so. But I am really out of practice with duelling-pistols."

Ajanta gave a little cry.

"What are you talking about?" she asked.

She slipped her arm through the Marquis's in an affectionate gesture that she knew Lord Burnham would note.

"You cannot be talking seriously," she said turning her blue eyes up to the Marquis's face. "If I thought you were going to do anything so terrible as to fight a duel, I should die through sheer fear that you might be injured."

"It was only a joke between Lord Burnham and myself," the Marquis said soothingly.

"But. .frightening," Ajanta said reproachfully. "I am sure Lord Burnham was really going to wish that we shall be very. .very. .happy, as we. .will be!"

She laid her cheek for a moment against the Marquis's shoulder.

As if he could bear no more, Lord Burnham gave an audible snort and turning walked towards the door.

When he reached it he looked back to say:

"Good day, Miss Tiverton, and I hope your happiness

will last! Stowe, I will keep certain papers until your wedding, when I will send them to you as a present."

With that he walked out of the room and slammed the door behind him.

CHAPTER SIX

The significance of what Lord Burnham had said took a moment or two to percolate into Ajanta's mind.

Then she realised that he must be referring to documents relating to the divorce, and this meant Lady Burnham and the Marquis would not be free of danger until he had actually married.

For a moment she felt that she could not have heard correctly what Lord Burnham had said, but the scowl on the Marquis's face and the tightness of his lips told her that he was well aware who after all, was the winner of the contest.

She stood still looking at him apprehensively, wondering what she could say.

She was aware with one part of her mind that Charis and Lyle were chattering on, yet she found it impossible to understand what they were saying.

Then as the Marquis looked at her and she knew he was going to say something important, the door opened and the Butler announced:

"Tea is served, My Lord, in the Blue Drawing-Room."

"Tea!" Darice exclaimed excitedly. "I hope there are more of those delicious little chocolate cakes."

Ajanta took her by the hand and they walked towards the Blue Drawing-Room and only when they had reached it did she realise that the Marquis had left them.

Her father was however waiting for her and as she poured out his tea he said:

"I have arranged with Quintus to go to Oxford tomorrow

and make arrangements to stay at my old College for at least a week. I suppose Lyle, you would not like to accompany me?"

The Vicar spoke with a smile on his lips as if he knew the answer before Lyle exclaimed:

"Oh, no, Papa! I have no wish to go back until I have to. I want to ride the horses here, and of course explore the grounds."

"I thought that would be your answer," the Vicar said complacently, "but it would be nice for me to see something of you when you return."

"Yes, of course, Papa," Lyle agreed.

But Ajanta knew that he was thinking that his interests and his father's were very far apart.

The Vicar was so excited with the thought of the research he could do on his book and the friends he would see again, that he talked of little else all through tea.

It was difficult for Ajanta to concentrate on what was being said, for she was thinking of the Marquis and realising the predicament he was in.

"He should never have suggested a. .pretend engagement. .in the first place," she told herself.

It had seemed a sensible idea at first, and it was only Lord Burnham's instinct which told him however convincing they had sounded, there was something wrong.

So now, at the very last moment he had played a trump card on the Marquis's ace.

"What am I to do. .now?" Ajanta asked. "What. .am I to do?"

It seemed as if the question turned itself over and over again in her mind, and however hard she tried, there seemed to be no answer.

At last tea came to an end, and as there was no sign of the Marquis Lyle said he would take Charis and Darice up to the top of the house and onto the roof.

"You will take care of them!" Ajanta said. "It might be dangerous."

126

"They will be safe with me," Lyle answered confidently, and left the Drawing-Room with his younger sisters chattering excitedly beside him.

The Vicar moved vaguely away and knowing that he was returning to the Library Ajanta decided that she must speak with the Marquis and ask him what he intended to do.

She knew that he would have gone to his private room which was exclusively his own and to which guests dared not intrude unless they were specifically invited.

She had heard him talking about this with her father and saying that if he had a Study, he had one too.

"Actually," he had confided, "it is where I read the newspapers and have a rest from the chatter of tongues and the tinkle of glasses."

The Vicar had laughed.

"You are very wise. Every man with any brains must have time to be alone with his thoughts and not be distracted by trivia."

"If you are referring to us, Papa," Ajanta interposed, "I resent being called 'trivia'!"

Her father had patted her arm.

"You know I like being alone with you, Ajanta, when we can talk seriously, but I find my family *en masse* is somewhat distracting."

Ajanta was sure that the Marquis now was avoiding all distractions while he thought things out and she walked rather nervously to where she knew his private Sitting-Room was situated.

Because she felt she was intruding she knocked on the door and when she heard his voice opened it and went in.

He was sitting in a high-backed arm-chair by the fireplace and when he saw her he looked surprised and rose to his feet.

"I thought I. .should come and. .talk to you," Ajanta said.

"I was in fact, going to suggest that you did that," the

Marquis replied. "Come in, Ajanta, and sit down."

She sat down on a chair facing his and he said:

"You understood what Burnham said as he was leaving?"

"I think he meant," Ajanta answered in a low voice, "that if you do not. .marry then he will go. .ahead with his. .divorce."

"Exactly!" the Marquis agreed.

"I am sorry. .really sorry that this should have. .happened," Ajanta said, "and Lady Burnham says she will. .kill herself if she is. .divorced."

The Marquis was astonished.

"You have seen her?"

"Yes," Ajanta replied. "She sent me an unsigned note this morning saying that you were in danger, and asking me to meet her on the other side of the wood in the Park."

"So that was why you took Mercury out alone!"

Ajanta nodded.

There was silence for a moment and now the Marquis said:

"You are now aware why I asked you to become engaged to me. I thought this afternoon, after Burnham had seen you that I had won and Lady Burnham and I would survive."

"That is. .what I. .thought too."

Ajanta gave a little sigh. Then added:

"I suppose Lord Burnham really. .meant what he said."

"He will certainly start divorce proceedings if I do not marry," the Marquis replied. "I can assure you it will give him immense pleasure to do so."

"Even though it will. .hurt and perhaps. .destroy his wife?"

"Burnham is thinking of nothing at the moment but destroying me!"

"What can. .we do?" Ajanta asked in a frightened voice.

Then before the Marquis could speak she said:

"I have an idea, although it might be difficult."

"What is it?" he asked in a somewhat uncompromising tone.

"As we have told so many lies," Ajanta answered, "I feel one more will not matter. I thought if you announced our marriage had taken place in Paris or somewhere else abroad, you could wait for Lord Burnham's papers to arrive. Then you could say I had had an. .unfortunate accident. .and I was. .dead."

The Marquis stared at her.

"It would not be. .very different," Ajanta went on. "We could have to take the family into our confidenced, at least Papa and Lyle, but if I went back to live quietly at the Vicarage I am sure Lord Burnham would not know where to find me."

"What would be our reason for being married abroad?"

"That is easy," Ajanta replied. "You could say we did not want all the fuss of a large wedding, which would have to be held here as my home is too small."

She thought for a moment. Then she continued:

"Your friends will all think quite reasonably that I am embarrassed at knowing so few people because I am of so little. .consequence."

She made a rather helpless little gesture with her hands.

"It will take a lot of. .thinking out. .but I am sure you could. .organise something like that very successfully. .and once I am. .presumed dead Lord Burnham will no. .longer be able to. .menace you."

The Marquis rose from his chair and walked across the room to stand at the window.

Ajanta watched him, thinking how large and strong he looked. With his body silhouetted against the sunshine he was also slim, athletic and she had to admit, very attractive.

"There is a much easier way out of this trouble," the Marquis said, "but I hesitate to suggest it."

"Why?" Ajanta enquired.

"Because you may not like it."

"What is your solution?"

"It is that you should marry me!"

For a moment she thought she could not have heard him aright.

Then she said quickly without thinking:

"No. .of course. .not! How could I possibly do. .that when you. .love Lady Burnham? And anyway, if you are to be married it should be to somebody of. . importance. .someone from your. .own world."

The Marquis did not reply but only stood still with his back to her.

As Ajanta finished speaking she felt her heart beating in a strange manner and quite suddenly she was aware almost as if she had been struck by lightning that she would in fact, like to marry the Marquis.

She was so astonished at her discovery that for a moment she felt she must be going mad.

Then she knew she loved him and had been irresistibly attracted to him from the very first moment she saw him.

It was now an unbearable agony to know that he loved Lady Burnham and she could mean nothing to him except as a lifeline to save them both from disaster.

It flashed through her mind like a series of pictures that when he had picked up Charis in the road after the accident he had been on his way to Dawlish Castle!

She was sure without being told that to save himself from the divorce case he had intended originally to marry Lady Sarah.

By a million to one chance, or perhaps it was the manipulation of Fate, he had come to the Vicarage and decided a 'pretence engagement' was a considerably more pleasant prospect than being tied for life to a woman he did not love.

"That is what.happened," Ajanta told herself.

Now everything had gone wrong!

The third act of the Marquis's Play was far from ending happily with the hero freed from his encumbrance and able to enjoy himself unrestrainedly.

Instead he might have to marry the leading lady,

although she was not the heroine and never had been!

"How could I have become involved in such a tangle?" Ajanta asked herself and was sure the Marquis was thinking the same.

She looked at him and knew, now that she had admitted her love for him, she had been very obtuse not to realise that everything she had told herself she felt about him was as false as their engagement.

It had been an indescribable delight to duel with him in words and realise for the first time in her life that she was talking to a man as an equal and holding her own intellectually.

At the same time she had been aware that her co-actor was the most attractive, and when he wished, the most charming man it was possible to imagine.

"Of course I fell in love with him!" she thought despairingly, "just as dozens of women as beautiful as Lady Burnham have done in the past and will do in the future."

Yet desperate to save the woman he loved and himself the Marquis had now asked her to marry him.

Ajanta suddenly thought how easy it would be to say 'Yes!'

Even if he did not care for her she would be near him, she would see him, she would bear his name.

Then she told herself it would not only destroy her dreams of love and her ideals, but also it would be a torture that she would rather die than endure.

Because she loved the Marquis he must never be aware of it. It would not only be the final humiliation for her, but it would also be extremely embarrassing for him.

Having made what was to all intents and purposes a business deal, they must find a business-like way out of their difficulties, without anyone except herself, and she did not count, being hurt in the process.

Because she found the whole idea so depressing Ajanta managed to say in a voice that trembled a little:

"I. .I think. .my solution is the best. .and I am

sure. .because you are so. .clever. .that you will find some way to. .make it work."

The Marquis did not reply and she went on:

"It is hard now that we are both. .upset to think clearly. .but at least we have a little time. .in which to do so."

She thought wildly as she spoke that no time could be too long as far as she was concerned.

She could for the time being see him, hear him and she could stay with him either here or in London, and it would be a wonder and a joy which she would be able to remember in the empty years ahead.

"I love you!" she wanted to say aloud, "and it will not. .matter to me. .how long we have to. .remain engaged."

It flashed through her mind that perhaps the Marquis could contrive to steal the incriminating papers from Lord Burnham.

Then she thought they would be with his Solicitors, so that would be impossible.

'We shall just have to go on pretending,' she thought.

Because she felt she could not bear to discuss it any further and the Marquis did not turn from the window, she walked swiftly across the room and left him without looking back.

She ran upstairs to her own room feeling that for the moment it was a sanctuary where she could be alone.

As she did so she thought that if she did stay with the Marquis for long, now that she loved him, it would be a very bitter-sweet pleasure.

Sweet because he was there, bitter because knowing who he loved she kept seeing Lady Burnham's beautiful face in front of her eyes.

'They are perfectly suited to each other,' Ajanta thought, 'and I suppose the best thing I could do would be to pray that Lord Burnham will die, then they could marry each other and be really happy.'

It was the sort of unselfish wish, she thought, that anyone who was really good would have. But she knew that although she loved the Marquis with all her heart, she did not want to think of him kissing and touching Lady Burnham.

Altogether she felt unbearably confused and bewildered by everything that had happened.

When she reached her bedroom she found Elsie laying out an evening-gown for her to wear.

"Oh, there you are, Miss!" she exclaimed. "I was hoping you'd come upstairs early."

"Why?" Ajanta enquired.

"Because Her Ladyship's arrived and is asking to see you, if it's convenient."

"Her. .Ladyship?"

"His Lordship's mother, the Marchioness," Elsie explained. "She was to have been here when you arrived, but she wasn't feeling well."

"But she is here now?"

"Her Ladyship came over from the Dower House about half-an-hour ago. She went straight to her room and'll be pleased if you'll go to her, Miss."

"Yes. .of course," Ajanta replied.

She knew there was nothing she could do but agree, however it would be embarrassing.

Yet if she had to act a lie to the Marquis's mother, it would be worse if he was present, especially at this moment when they were both stunned by Lord Burnham's ultimatum.

As Ajanta followed Elsie down the corridor to the South wing the maid remarked:

"These rooms are always kept ready for Her Ladyship."

There was no need for Ajanta to reply for as she spoke Elsie knocked on a large mahogany door, and it was opened a few seconds later by an elderly lady's-maid.

"I've brought Miss Tiverton to see Her Ladyship," Elsie explained.

"Thank you, Elsie. Will you come in, Miss?"

Ajanta stepped into a small Hall and the maid opened another door.

"Miss Ajanta Tiverton, M'Lady!" she announced.

Because sunshine seemed to fill the room it was difficult at first for Ajanta to see its occupant.

Then she realised that in a bow window at the far end there was a woman with white hair, sitting in a wheel-chair.

Ajanta moved towards her, thinking perhaps after all she should have waited for the Marquis, and his mother might think it strange for her to come alone.

"I am so delighted to meet you," a soft voice said. "You must forgive me for not being here when you arrived, but I have these tiresome bouts of pain when it is impossible for me to move about."

"I am sorry," Ajanta said.

She had reached the wheel-chair by this time and as she curtsied and held out her hand the Marchioness gave a little cry!

"You cannot be!" she exclaimed. "And yet – you must be – Margaret's daughter!"

Ajanta stared at her.

"In fact, you are so like her," the Marchioness went on, "that I thought for one incredible moment that the years had rolled back and you were your mother!"

"You. .knew Mama?"

It was difficult for Ajanta to speak, she was so surprised. The Marchioness smiled.

"We were at School together and she was my greatest friend. I was to be her bride's-maid when she ran away with your father."

Ajanta stood staring at the Marchioness feeling that in a day of surprises once again it was hard to think.

As she was silent the Marchioness went on:

"I feel because my son did not mention your mother she must be dead."

"Y.yes. .she died two years ago," Ajanta said in a low voice.

"I am so sorry," the Marchioness said. "I have thought of her so often and wondered what happened to her. You see, when your grandfather was so angry and refused to have her name ever mentioned again by the family or any of her friends, we had no idea what happened."

"Mama and Papa hid themselves after. .Papa had been. .threatened that he would be. .horse-whipped."

The Marchioness gave an exclamation.

"That sounds very like your grandfather. The Earl of Winsdale was a very autocratic and intimidating man when he was young, but now he is old, nearly blind, and rather pathetic."

Ajanta had been listening almost as if she was hypnotised by the Marchioness and now she said:

"Please. .Ma'am. .may I ask you. .something? It is very. .very important."

"Of course, dear. I hope nothing I have said has upset you."

"Actually it has," Ajanta answered. "You see, Ma'am, I am the only one in the family who. .knows who Mama. . was."

"You mean your brother and sisters have not been told that she ran away with your father?"

Without really thinking what she was doing Ajanta knelt down beside the Marchioness's chair.

She thought as she did so that the Marquis's mother had a very sweet and kind face. At the same time it was beautiful even though lined with pain.

"I expect, Ma'am, you know," she began, "when Papa fell in love with my mother she was engaged to somebody very important, of whom her family approved."

The Marchioness smiled.

"Yes, I knew about that."

"Mama asked her father if she could break off her engagement, but he was very angry."

135

The Marchioness nodded.

"I am sure he was, and the Earl's anger was very frightening."

"Mama was terrified, and when Papa stood up to him and said they were determined to be married, he had him thrown out of the house bodily and threatened with a horse-whip if he ever returned."

"I did not know that," the Marchioness said, "but I knew they ran away."

"Mama said that. .nothing should come between them and their. .love," Ajanta went on, her voice softening, "and so they hid until Papa managed to persuade the Duke of Dawlish's father, who had been kind to him when he was a boy, to give him a living on his estate. He did not know who Papa had married, and the present Duke has no idea either."

"They were happy?" the Marchioness asked.

"Very, very happy, and so much in love."

"And now Margaret's daughter is to marry my son!" the Marchioness exclaimed. "I cannot tell you how happy that makes me!"

As she spoke Ajanta was suddenly aware that this had brought a new complexity into her already complicated position with the Marquis.

He had asked her to be really married to him as a solution to his problem.

She had made the suggestion that somehow she could disappear or appear to have died to save him from being tied to a wife he did not want.

If he knew that her grandfather was the Earl of Winsdale and her mother had been his mother's closest friend, he would feel obliged to marry her, whatever his feelings in the matter.

At the moment she was an obscure, unimportant nobody, but as her mother's daughter she was in fact somebody in the social world in which he moved.

Looking up into the Marchioness's face Ajanta said quickly:

"Please, Ma'am, please give me your word of honour that you will not mention to the Marquis or anybody else that you knew Mama or anything about her. I cannot. .explain, but at the. .moment this. .must be kept a. .secret."

The Marchioness looked bewildered, then she said:

"I expect you are afraid of upsetting your father, but of course I hope that there will be no secrets between you and my son."

She waited for Ajanta to speak and when she did not do so, she said:

"I understand, you want to tell him in your own time, and therefore I promise you, my dear, that I will not say anything until you allow me to do so."

"Thank you, thank you!" Ajanta cried.

The Marchioness looked down at her with a very soft expression in her eyes.

"You are everything I wanted in my son's wife," she said. "I have prayed that he would find the right girl, and not one of those London women I find hard and brittle and who have no conception of real love or how wonderful it can be."

She put out her hand to touch Ajanta's cheek softly:

"You are so beautiful, and I know that you and Quintus will be very, very happy together, just as you say your father and mother found happiness despite all they had to suffer."

Her words brought the tears to Ajanta's eyes.

"Kiss me, my dearest child," the Marchioness said, "and now I know it is time for you to dress for dinner. Tomorrow I hope to be feeling well enough to come downstairs to meet your father and the rest of your family."

"They will love to meet you."

"Thank you," the Marchioness smiled. "I look forward to having a long talk with you when I am a little stronger but do not worry, I will keep your secret."

Back in her own bedroom Ajanta felt her head whirling.

How could she have imagined, how could she have known that after all these years she would meet one of her mother's friends, who by an extraordinary coincidence was the mother of the man she was supposed to be marrying?

"He must never. .never know," she told herself fiercely, "and I shall never. .never. .marry."

She went to the window to look at the swans on the lake and the sun sinking behind the trees.

Tonight it seemed lovelier than it had ever been before and the beauty of it tempted her.

"All this could be yours," it said, "yours for ever."

The house itself was saying the same words, and the room in which she was standing with the goddesses and the cupids on the ceiling were joining in.

She could see herself living here with the Marquis and perhaps, because he would think it his duty, he would kiss her, hold her in his arms, and perhaps even sleep with her on the bed with its lace and silk hangings.

Then, although her lips did not move she heard a voice ring out from her heart and her soul saying clearly unmistakably until the sound of it vibrated high into the sky:

"No! Not without love! Never, never without love!"

. . . .

When Ajanta had left his private room the Marquis had turned from the window to stare at the door she had closed behind her.

Then he walked to his desk and rang a gold bell which summoned his secretary from the office next door.

"Has the jeweller arrived, Clements?" the Marquis asked the pleasant-faced man of about forty who had looked after his affairs for over ten years.

"Yes, My Lord. He's waiting until it is convenient for Your Lordship to see him."

"Send him in," the Marquis said, "and as I have a little extra work for him to do he will undoubtedly have to stay the night."

"I have already anticipated that might be the case, Your Lordship," Mr. Clements replied.

He went to fetch the jeweller and the Marquis sat deep in thought until the man arrived.

. . . .

A short while later the Marquis went upstairs to greet his mother.

By the time he reached the south wing she was in bed looking very attractive in a becoming little lace cap trimmed with bows of blue ribbon over her white hair and a shawl of the same lace lined with satin over her shoulders.

"Dearest Quintus!" she exclaimed as the Marquis entered the room. "I am so sorry I have been so tiresome and could not come as soon as you required me to do so."

"You are here now and that is all that matters," the Marquis answered. "How are you, Mama?"

He kissed his mother's hand and then her cheek and sat down on the side of her bed, still holding her hand in his.

"I have seen Ajanta," the Marchioness said, "and, Quintus, she is adorable! Just the sort of wife I wished you to find."

"I am glad you think that, Mama."

"How could you have been so clever as to discover such a beautiful and charming girl? I shall look forward to meeting the rest of her family tomorrow."

"You will like them all."

"I have prayed and prayed that you would be married to somebody you loved," the Marchioness went on, "and now my prayers have been answered. I am just wondering how I can express my gratitude to God and of course to you for being so clever."

"You can do that quite easily, Mama, by getting well," the Marquis replied. "You know how it upsets me when you are in pain."

"I know, dearest, but I have a feeling that since now I am so happy about you, that I shall feel better than I have for a long time."

Her fingers clung to his as she said:

"I have been so worried about you these last two years. Your life seemed so aimless and was such a waste of your intelligence."

The Marquis looked surprised.

"I had no idea that you felt like that, Mama."

The Marchioness smiled.

"You can be quite certain there were plenty of people to tell me who was your latest acquisition, and they succeeded each other very rapidly."

The Marquis laughed.

"There is one thing about you, Mama, you are always well informed!"

"It has not always made me very happy," the Marchioness replied. "Then when I felt almost in despair when I heard about your association with the beautiful Lady Burnham, you surprise and delight me by producing this exquisite creature who might have stepped out of a story-book."

"She is certainly very beautiful," the Marquis agreed.

"And intelligent!"

The Marquis smiled.

"Sometimes I think too much so. You will hardly believe it, Mama, but she actually argues with me!"

The Marchioness laughed.

"Can there exist a woman who does not agree with everything you say being convinced that you must always be right?"

"Wait until you know Ajanta a little better."

"That is what I intend to do," the Marchioness replied, "and if she can make you exercise your very good brain and

140

prevent it from becoming fat and lazy, then I shall know that those quickly-fading love-affairs are a thing of the past."

The Marquis rose from the bed.

"Both you and Ajanta frighten me, Mama," he said, "and if you combine forces then I shall feel I can no longer go on fighting for my supremacy but will have to surrender to you unconditionally."

"That is what we must make sure of," the Marchioness laughed.

The Marquis kissed her and left.

As he went to change for dinner he found himself thinking of several ways in which he could defeat Ajanta in the arguments which he was quite certain she would be waiting to have with him either tonight or tomorrow.

"How can she be so beautiful and so clever?" he asked.

Then he remembered Ajanta had already answered that question in one word – love.

CHAPTER SEVEN

"It has been a fantastic day," Lyle said as he kissed Ajanta goodbye. "I have never enjoyed myself so much!"

The young men with him all said the same thing and Ajanta noticed the admiring looks they gave the Marquis as they enthused over his horses.

It had, Ajanta thought, been one of the happiest days she herself had ever spent and she knew it was because Lyle's excitement was infectious.

She was aware how much it meant to him to bring his friends over from Oxford and for them to be able to ride the Marquis's superb horses round the race-track and also take part in a point-to-point which he arranged for them.

The excellent luncheon to which they did full justice, and the excitement of Charis and Darice was all part of Ajanta's contentment.

'If only this could go on for ever,' she thought, but knew the future was waiting like a dark shadow to dim the sunshine.

Lyle had reached the front door when he put his hand into the pocket of his coat and exclaimed:

"I nearly forgot! Papa told me to give you this."

He put a small book into Ajanta's hands saying:

"Here are some Greek poems he has found and he is quite sure you will enjoy them as much as he did."

"I shall!" Ajanta exclaimed.

Then she realised that the Marquis was listening and added:

"I should not say so in front of His Lordship! He does not approve of women who can read Greek and Latin and thinks I am becoming a 'blue-stocking'."

"If he disapproves," Lyle said in mock dismay, "I had best take it straight back to Papa."

"No, no, of course not!" Ajanta laughed, holding the book tightly to prevent him from taking it from her.

Nevertheless when she waved goodbye to her brother and his friends she thought of the lovely Lady Burnham and was quite certain she did not read Greek, Latin, or perhaps anything except the social columns of the newspapers.

Lyle and his friends had had an early dinner before they returned to Oxford, and now Ajanta started to climb the staircase knowing that Darice had gone to bed before dinner and Charis was saying good-night to the Marchioness.

She was half-way up the stairs when the Marquis said:

"When you have said goodnight to my mother, Ajanta, which is where I am imagine you are going now, I would like to speak to you in my Study."

"Yes, of course."

Ajanta tried to smile as she spoke, but her heart sank as she wished that this was not to be the end of what had been such a perfect day.

There had been so much to do in the last forty-eight hours that there had not been a second for what she knew must be the inevitable talk with the Marquis when he would decide her future.

"Why can we not go on as we are now?" she asked despairingly.

The answer lay with Lord Burnham who was the ogre in her fairy-tale, threatening the Marquis not with death but with the scandal of his divorce proceedings.

Last night when Ajanta had gone to bed with the laughter of her family still ringing in her ears she had asked herself once again if she should not sink her pride and accept the Marquis's suggestion that they should be properly married.

It was impossible not to keep thinking of how much she

could do for those she loved!

But all the suggestions being made for their well-being she knew – were like a card-castle which would collapse at the first breath of wind.

This morning the Marchioness had said to her:

"I have been thinking, dearest Ajanta, that when you and Quintus are married, it would be a mistake for you not to be alone together. I am therefore hoping you will let me have your two sisters to live with me at the Dower House. It is so near that you could see them as much as you wished and I think they would be happy with me."

"I know they would be, Ma'am," Ajanta replied.

Darice had already attached herself to the Marchioness and had even said to Ajanta:

"She is so understanding. When I am talking to her it is like being with Mama."

Almost as if she was thought-reading, the Marchioness had continued:

"I think it would be in Charis's best interests for her to go for at least six months to a good finishing school, and what could be better than the one which your mother and I attended and where we were very happy?"

Ajanta had to agree. At the same time she knew it was all wishful thinking and that when she had to disappear all these plans would come to an end.

Then they would be back at the Vicarage with nothing to do except talk about what 'might have been.'

"I love him! How can I bear never to see him again?" she asked in the darkness of the night.

Then once again she saw Lady Burnham's beautiful face and knew that to live with the Marquis, loving him as she did, and know he was thinking not of her, but of another woman would be to suffer all the tortures of the damned.

"I have to do what is right," she told herself. "To marry just for position and money would be wrong and wicked however much it would benefit the family."

She thought that perhaps because the Marquis was so

kind he might allow them to keep the horses he had promised Charis and Darice, and might sometimes let Lyle come over to Stowe from Oxford.

He would see the Marquis and talk to him while to her he would be lost for ever and she would only have her memories of him.

As she expected, when she reached the Marchioness's room Charis was sitting beside the bed and Ajanta heard her laughter ring out as she entered.

"I was just telling Her Ladyship what a wonderful, exciting, happy day we have had," Charis said when her sister appeared, "and it is all due to me! I found your future husband for you!"

"Yes, you did," Ajanta agreed.

"It is the luckiest accident that ever happened!" Charis exclaimed.

"I think so too," the Marchioness said in her soft voice. "And now, as I am sure there will be another happy day tomorrow, I think, Charis, you should go to bed and dream about all the compliments which Lyle's friends paid you."

"I think really they were complimenting the horse I was riding," Charis smiled, "but I liked to hear them all the same."

She bent forward, kissed the Marchioness goodnight, saying:

"Thank you, thank you for being so kind. May I come and talk to you tomorrow? I still have lots more things to tell you."

"Yes, of course, dearest child. I shall look forward to it," the Marchioness replied.

Charis kissed Ajanta, then went from the room.

When she had gone the Marchioness said:

"Your sister will be very lovely in a year's time and you must certainly give a Ball for her here, and another in London."

Ajanta drew in her breath, but before she could reply the Marchioness went on:

"I was thinking today when I was watching your sisters and Lyle's young friends from Oxford, that what Quintus missed as a child was not having any brothers and sisters. I have always regretted so bitterly that after he was born I was unable to have any more children."

The inference of what the Marchioness was saying was obvious but there was nothing Ajanta could say in reply.

She could only think that nothing would be more marvellous than to have the Marquis's children, and know that she could make his life as full and happy as theirs had been when her mother was alive.

"It has been a delightful day," the Marchioness said with a sigh, "but now I admit to feeling a little tired. Yet because there is so much I want to do with your two adorable sisters, I am determined to get well. In fact I am certain I feel better already."

"I will pray very hard that you will be," Ajanta answered.

She kissed the Marchioness and said goodnight, but did not realise as she went from the room that the older woman looked after her with a worried expression in her eyes, sensing there was something wrong, but unable to think what it could possibly be.

Ajanta went slowly down the stairs.

She could not escape from the miserable feeling that she was about to reach the end of the fairy-story and no one was going to live happily ever after.

'At least I shall have it all to remember,' she thought as she reached the marble Hall.

Then she walked more and more slowly down the passage which led to the Marquis's private Study.

She felt as if she was already saying goodbye to the pictures, to the furniture, to the house itself, which she thought in some strange way had become part of herself, although of course, that was a ridiculous idea!

She paused outside the Study door, drew in her breath and instinctively, because she knew she had to be very

146

resolute, her chin went up and she walked in.

She expected the Marquis to be sitting at his desk, but instead he was standing in front of the mantelpiece waiting for her.

She shut the door behind her, but though she knew that his eyes were on her as she walked towards him, she found herself unable to look at him.

She wanted to speak naturally but, when she reached him and stopped a few feet in front of him, her voice seemed to have died in her throat and she could only wait.

"We seem to have been so busy yesterday and today," the Marquis said after what seemed a long pause, "that there has been no time, Ajanta, for us to finish our conversation."

"No," she murmured.

"I think you will remember, that I made a suggestion to you, and you made one to me, and I think we should come to some decision as to which we accept."

"Y.yes. .of course," Ajanta replied.

Because she was near the Marquis, because she knew how handsome and attractive he was looking in his evening-clothes, she felt as if every nerve in her body vibrated towards him.

Yet at the same time she felt as if she loved him so overwhelmingly that it sapped her will and she felt helpless and ready to do anything he asked of her.

"I have to be sensible," she told herself. "I have to remember that he does not love me."

"Shall we discuss your suggestion first?" the Marquis was saying in a voice she thought sounded firm and business-like.

Ajanta nodded, for it was impossible for her to speak.

"Your idea was," the Marquis went on, "that we should pretend to have been married abroad, and thus obtain the incriminating papers from Lord Burnham with which he has threatened me. Then we should announce that there had been an unfortunate accident and you were dead."

The Marquis waited for Ajanta to speak, and when she did not do so, he continued:

"As you pointed out, this would involve taking your father and Lyle into our confidence, and I think you would find that Charis would ask a great many awkward questions."

Ajanta clasped her fingers together. Her voice seemed to come unsteadily from a long distance as she said:

"We could. .explain to. .Charis that we were not. .suited to each other, and there would be. .nothing she could. .do but. .accept the situation."

"I suppose not," the Marquis said doubtfully. "At the same time, it would be very hard for her to understand why you should refuse to marry me when all your family, I think, found new interests here at Stowe."

"Of course they. .have," Ajanta replied, "and you have been so very. .very. .kind to them."

She thought her voice trembled almost as if she was near to tears, and went on quickly:

"It has been. .wonderful for all of us to stay in such a. .magnificent house. .to ride your horses. .and to see a world that before only existed in our imagination. .but it has to come to an. .end and there is. .nothing any of us can do. .about it."

"That is not true," the Marquis said sharply. "You can marry me, as I suggested you should do, and then it would be yours and theirs for ever."

"You. .know that is. .impossible!" Ajanta murmured.

"Why?"

"Because I cannot make you. .happy. .You. .love somebody else. .and it would be wrong. .completely and absolutely wrong for me to. .ruin your life if there is an. . alternative."

"You are thinking of me?"

"Of course I am! I have seen. .Lady Burnham and I know. .what she. .means to you. The only thing I can do to. .save you is to. .disappear."

148

"At whatever the cost to your family and yourself?"

He was making it very difficult, Ajanta thought, but still she dared not look at him. Holding herself very stiffly and forcing the words between her lips, she answered:

"You came into our. .lives just by. .chance. If there had been no accident and Charis had not been there, we would never have. .met you. It has been more. .wonderful than I can possibly. .explain to have known you. .but now you have to think of yourself. .and your future. .happiness."

"And you really believe you can put back the clock?" the Marquis asked. "In giving up everything here you will have no regrets?"

"Of course we will have. .regrets. .and it will be. .difficult," Ajanta agreed. "Very difficult. At the same time. .we must do what is. .right for. .you."

There was another long pause.

"You are still thinking of me!" the Marquis repeated.

"Of course I am thinking of you!" Ajanta said forcefully. "You are so clever. .you are so. .intelligent. You can find your way out of this mess. .then perhaps later on you will fall in. .love with. .somebody you can marry and be. .really happy, as your mother wants. .you to be."

"My mother wants me to marry you," the Marquis said quietly.

"Her Ladyship does not. .understand," Ajanta said. "Naturally she thinks we are in love. .and she is happy. .so very happy. .that you should be married and have. .children to make Stowe a house of. .love."

Although she tried to speak calmly and sensibly she could not help her voice breaking on the last word.

Because she was so afraid she would betray her real feelings she turned and walked away from the Marquis as he had once done, to stand at the window looking out onto the twilight.

The last crimson and golden glow of the sun was vanishing behind the trees and the stars were coming out in the sky overhead.

149

The lake in the Park looked enchanted, and she thought with an agony of despair that to leave Stowe would be like leaving the Garden of Eden and being driven into the Wilderness.

Then the Marquis spoke again and she gave a little start since she had not realised he had followed her and was standing just behind her.

"What I cannot understand, Ajanta," he said, "is why you are thinking so much of me. After all, we have known each other a very short time, and as you have just pointed out, we only met by chance. Why should you be so concerned?"

"I. .I want you to be. .happy."

"Why?"

There was one obvious answer to that which Ajanta could not give, and because there was a note in the Marquis's voice which she had not heard before she felt herself tremble, and could only press her lips together in case she betrayed herself.

"I want you to answer that question," the Marquis said quietly.

With an effort Ajanta forced herself to say:

"Please. .we cannot go on. .talking about this. Just tell me what I am to do. .then I will carry out your. .instructions."

"Very well," the Marquis said, "if that is what you want. I have, as it happens, made my plans."

"I thought you. .would do. .that."

Because she could not bear to go on looking at the beauty of the twilight outside she turned round to look at the Marquis.

"Tell me what your. .plan is," she said in what she hoped was a calm, businesslike manner.

The Marquis walked to his desk and Ajanta feeling a little surprised followed him step by step.

"I have two things for you," he said. "First an engagement ring, which I should have given to you before and which I am sure our visitors of the last few days have expected to see on your finger."

As he spoke he opened a velvet case and Ajanta saw inside it there was a diamond ring that made her gasp.

A perfect stone surrounded by smaller diamonds seemed to her so large and so lovely that it was almost as if the Marquis had taken one of the stars from the sky and was holding it out for her inspection.

Then she remembered she could only wear it for a very short time, and when she disappeared it must be returned.

"I will put it on your finger in a moment," the Marquis said, still in the quiet voice in which he had spoken before, "but first I want you to try the wedding-ring I have chosen for you, just in case it is not the right size."

"Y.yes. .of course," Ajanta agreed.

It made her feel strange to hear him speak of giving her a wedding-ring. She thought he might have waited until they had reached Paris or wherever they were going for their pretence marriage.

At the same time, it was like his efficiency and his perfect organisation to have everything planned and in order.

The Marquis opened the other case and she saw inside that there was a gold ring.

He drew it out and held it between his first finger and thumb.

Because she was feeling shy and embarrassed, Ajanta asked:

"Have you. .decided where we are to be. .married and how long afterwards we should wait before I. .disappear?"

"That depends on you," the Marquis replied.

"On me?" Ajanta enquired.

As she spoke she thought of how every hour, every minute, every second she could be with him would be so precious that she would treasure them.

"Yes, on you," the Marquis said positively.

She looked at him with a puzzled expression in her eyes, but he was still looking at the wedding-ring.

"As a matter of fact," he said, "the answer to your question is written inside this ring, so I suggest you read it and see if you agree to do what I want."

Ajanta looked at him still puzzled, and now his eyes met hers.

She thought perhaps it was a trick of the light but his expression made her heart leap, then for no reason she could understand she was trembling.

"Before it is too dark for you to see," the Marquis said, "I suggest you read what I have had engraved inside this ring."

As he spoke he held it out towards her and as instinctively she put out her hand he placed it in her palm.

For a moment it was impossible to move, then with what was a superhuman effort she picked up the ring with her other hand and looked inside it.

In the dying light it was possible to see there were some words deeply engraved on the gold.

Slowly, almost as if her brain could not obey her, she read them out.

"FOR ALL ETERNITY"

For a second she felt her eyes must be deceiving her, and she could not be seeing right.

Then as she gave a little gasp the Marquis's arms went round her.

"That is my plan, Ajanta," he said. "The plan in which you have promised to obey me."

Because he was holding her Ajanta's heart felt as if it turned a dozen somersaults and was beating so frantically that it was impossible to think.

Somewhere, far away, she heard her voice stammer:

"Wh. .what are. .you. .saying? I do not. .understand!"

"I am saying that I love you," the Marquis said, "as I know you love me."

He put his hand under her chin and turned her face up to his.

152

"That is true, is it not?" he asked. "You could not be so unselfish, so unbelievably self-sacrificing unless you loved me?"

He did not wait for her to answer but his lips came down on hers, then he drew her close against him and his mouth held her captive.

To Ajanta it was as if she was swept from the darkness into a celestial light which filled the whole world and the sky above.

Then as the Marquis's lips became more insistent, more demanding, everything vanished except the closeness of him.

An unbelievable rapture flooded through her so that she felt she must have died and was no longer human, but part of the divine.

It was so perfect, so wonderful that Ajanta could only know that this was love, the love she had always sought, the love she believed in and which she had despaired of ever finding.

Only when the Marquis raised his head for a moment did she manage to say:

"I. .love. .you. .I love. .you. .but I never. .thought that you. .would love. .me."

"I think I have loved you from the very first moment I saw you," the Marquis said. "I told myself that you were too beautiful to be real, and far too clever to be the sort of wife I expected to marry."

"And. .now?" Ajanta whispered.

"Now I know I cannot live without you, and that I have no wish for a 'pretend' engagement, my darling, but a real marriage, and one that will last for all eternity."

"Do you. .mean that. .do you really. .mean it?"

"I knew when I had the ring engraved that you were everything that existed in a very sacred place in my heart, but which I thought would always remain empty."

Ajanta gave a little sob and turned her face against his shoulder.

"I. .I thought when I saw Lady. .Burnham that I could never. .mean anything to you."

"Forget her!" the Marquis said. "She is a very sweet and lovely person, but even if she were free I would not have asked her to be my wife."

Ajanta raised her head.

"Is that. .true?" she asked wonderingly.

The Marquis's arms tightened around her.

"Because we must always be honest with each other, my darling," he said, "I admit there have been a great many women in my life. But I was determined to be free and remain unmarried, simply because none of them were the woman I wanted to bring to Stowe, to live here with me and be the mother of my children."

He kissed Ajanta's forehead before he went on:

"When I saw you here in the house I knew you were exactly the person I had been looking for. You fitted in a way I cannot explain, except that I know you are the only woman I have ever met who could take my mother's place and also own a part of me which I have never given to anybody else."

Ajanta gave a little cry of happiness.

"That is what I want you to say," she said. "It is what Papa and Mama felt for each other and it is what I have always longed and prayed for but like you, thought I would never find."

As she spoke she thought that now she could tell the Marquis who her mother was, but it could wait.

"You have not met many men, my precious one, living where you did," the Marquis said.

"That is true, and yet Fate brought us together in the most unexpected way."

"Perhaps after all we neither of us, had enough faith in our own destiny," the Marquis said. "But now, my lovely one, we have found what we both know is the most precious thing on earth, and we will never lose it."

"Never! Never!" Ajanta cried.

The Marquis kissed her again.

She felt as if she gave him not only her lips and her heart but her body and her soul.

She was part of him and never again would she be alone and frightened, unhappy or afraid.

She pressed herself close and still closer and felt a strange fire in the Marquis's kiss.

It lit a fire within her breasts which burnt its way up her throat until it touched her lips and his.

"I worship you and I want you!" the Marquis said hoarsely. "I cannot wait to make you mine. We will be married here in the Chapel the day after tomorrow."

"Will not. .everyone think it rather. .strange?" Ajanta asked.

Her whole being was singing with happiness and the wonder and glory of having the Marquis love her.

"Does it matter what they think?" he asked.

"No,"

"Are you sure of that?"

"The only thing. .that matters. .is that you love me!. .You are sure I am. .not dreaming?"

"We both are," he answered, and kissed her again.

When they raised their heads the room was almost dark and he drew her to the window.

The stars were reflected in the lake, and as the moon rose up the sky, the shadows were deep, mysterious and exciting.

"Stowe is. .enchanted," Ajanta whispered.

"It always will be for us," the Marquis said as he kissed her hair.

She raised her face to his as she said:

"There is. .something I want to. .say to you."

"What is it?"

"Your house is enchanted, everything you do seems part of a fairy-story, but if. .like Mama and Papa. .we had to run away together. .to live in poverty and obscurity I would go with you willingly. .without for one

155

moment. .thinking it was any sacrifice."

The way she spoke was so very moving that the Marquis's arms tightened.

Then when she thought he would kiss her, he put his cheek against hers and said:

"That is why I know you love me, and because you are prepared to give up so much for me, there is nothing that I do not want to give you, even taking the stars and the moon from the sky, so that you can hold them in your arms."

"I have. .nothing to give you. .but my. .love."

"A love that fills the whole world," the Marquis answered. "A love, my darling, which will not only be ours now, but will grow, I believe, greater and more wonderful, every year we are together."

Then as the tears came into Ajanta's eyes from sheer happiness, the Marquis was kissing her again.

Kissing her until she felt that he really had taken the stars and the moon from the sky for her to hold against her breasts.

She knew that the love they had for each other was greater than either of them could ever express and was the love which came from God and belonged to God, and would be theirs for all eternity.

THE END

THE PROUD PRINCESS
by BARBARA CARTLAND

From Barbara Cartland, one of the most romantic and internationally famous writers, comes the touching story of a young and beautiful Princess whose pride would not allow her to love. . . .

0 552 10229 6   95p

A PORTRAIT OF LOVE
by BARBARA CARTLAND

From Barbara Cartland, comes an exciting new story about the beautiful but impoverished Fedora Colwyn, who plans to help her sick father pay off the family debts but instead finds herself implicated in a murder.

0 552 11876 1   95p

A TOUCH OF LOVE
by BARBARA CARTLAND

From Barbara Cartland, one of the most romantic and internationally famous writers, comes a moving tale of a girl who softened the heart of a tyrant with a touch of love.

0 552 10744 1   95p

A SELECTION OF BARBARA CARTLAND TITLES AVAILABLE IN CORGI PAPERBACK

While every effort is made to keep prices low, it is sometimes necessary to increase prices at short notice. Corgi Books reserve the right to show new retail prices on covers which may differ from those previously advertised in the text or elsewhere.

The prices shown below were correct at the time of going to press.

☐	11787 0	**DOLLARS FOR THE DUKE**	*Barbara Cartland* 95p
☐	11840 0	**WINGED MAGIC**	*Barbara Cartland* 95p
☐	10169 9	**NEVER LAUGH AT LOVE**	*Barbara Cartland* 95p
☐	10168 0	**A DREAM FROM THE NIGHT**	*Barbara Cartland* 95p
☐	10228 8	**THE SECRET OF THE GLEN**	*Barbara Cartland* 95p
☐	11876 1	**A PORTRAIT OF LOVE**	*Barbara Cartland* 95p
☐	10229 6	**THE PROUD PRINCESS**	*Barbara Cartland* 95p
☐	10255 5	**HUNGRY FOR LOVE**	*Barbara Cartland* 95p
☐	10786 7	**NO ESCAPE FROM LOVE**	*Barbara Cartland* 95p
☐	10305 5	**THE DISGRACEFUL DUKE**	*Barbara Cartland* 95p
☐	10602 X	**PUNISHMENT OF A VIXEN**	*Barbara Cartland* 95p
☐	11930 X	**A SHAFT OF SUNLIGHT**	*Barbara Cartland* 95p
☐	10549 X	**A DUEL WITH DESTINY**	*Barbara Cartland* 95p
☐	11136 8	**WHO CAN DENY LOVE**	*Barbara Cartland* 95p
☐	10690 9	**THE LOVE PIRATE**	*Barbara Cartland* 95p
☐	10744 1	**A TOUCH OF LOVE**	*Barbara Cartland* 95p
☐	11045 0	**LOVE CLIMBS IN**	*Barbara Cartland* 95p
☐	11097 3	**A NIGHTINGALE SANG**	*Barbara Cartland* 95p

ORDER FORM

All these books are available at your book shop or newsagent, or can be ordered direct from the publisher. Just tick the titles you want and fill in the form below.

CORGI BOOKS, Cash Sales Department, P.O. Box 11, Falmouth, Cornwall.

Please send cheque or postal order, no currency.

Please allow cost of book(s) plus the following for postage and packing:

U.K. Customers—Allow 45p for the first book, 20p for the second book and 14p for each additional book ordered, to a maximum charge of £1.63.

B.F.P.O. and Eire—Allow 45p for the first book, 20p for the second book plus 14p per copy for the next 7 books, thereafter 8p per book.

Overseas Customers—Allow 75p for the first book and 21p per copy for each additional book.

NAME (Block Letters) ....

ADDRESS ....

....

(June '82)